Bad Best Friend

Billionaire's Club #14

Elise Faber

BAD BEST FRIEND
BY ELISE FABER
Newsletter sign-up

This is a work of fiction. Names, places, characters, and events are fictitious in every regard. Any similarities to actual events and persons, living or dead, are purely coincidental. Any trademarks, service marks, product names, or named features are assumed to be the property of their respective owners, and are used only for reference. There is no implied endorsement if any of these terms are used. Except for review purposes, the reproduction of this book in whole or part, electronically or mechanically, constitutes a copyright violation.

BAD BEST FRIEND
Copyright © 2022 Elise Faber
Print ISBN-13: 978-1-63749-042-6
Ebook ISBN-13: 978-1-63749-041-9
Cover Art by Jena Brignola

Billionaire's Club

Bad Night Stand

Bad Breakup

Bad Husband

Bad Hookup

Bad Divorce

Bad Fiancé

Bad Boyfriend

Bad Blind Date

Bad Wedding

Bad Engagement

Bad Bridesmaid

Bad Swipe

Bad Girlfriend

Bad Best Friend

Bad Rebound

Billionaire's Club Cast of Characters

Heroes and Heroines:

Abigail Roberts (Bad Night Stand) — founding member of the Sextant, hates wine, loves crocheting
Jordan O'Keith (Bad Night Stand) — Heather's brother, former owner of RoboTech
Cecilia (CeCe) Thiele (Bad Breakup) — former nanny to Hunter, talented artist
Colin McGregor (Bad Breakup) — Scottish duke, owner of McGregor Enterprises
Heather O'Keith (Bad Husband) — CEO of RoboTech, Jordan's sister
Clay Steele (Bad Husband) — Heather's business rival, CEO of Steele Technologies
Kay (Bad Date) — romance writer, hates to be stood up
Garret Williams (Bad Date) — former rugby player
Rachel Morris (Bad Hookup) — Heather's assistant, superpowers include being ultra-organized

Sebastian (Bas) Scott (Bad Hookup) — Devon Scott's brother, Clay's assistant
Rebecca (Bec) Darden (Bad Divorce) — kickass lawyer, New York roots
Luke Pearson (Bad Divorce) — Southern gentleman, CEO Pearson Energies
Seraphina Delgado (Bad Fiancé) — romantic to the core, looks like a bombshell, but even prettier on the inside
Tate Connor (Bad Fiancé) — tech genius, scared to be burned by love
Lorelai (Bad Text) — drunk texts don't make her happy
Logan Smith (Bad Text) — former military, sometimes drunk texts are for the best
Kelsey Scott (Bad Boyfriend) — Bas and Devon's sister, engineer at RoboTech, brilliant
Tanner Pearson (Bad Boyfriend) — Bas and Devon's childhood friend, photographer
Trix Donovan (Bad Blind Date) — Heather's sister, Jordan's half-sister, nurse who worked in war zones, poverty-stricken areas, and abroad for almost a decade
Jet Hansen (Bad Blind Date) — a doctor Trix worked with
Molly Miller (Bad Wedding) — owner of Molly's, a kickass bakery in San Francisco
Jackson Davis (Bad Wedding) — Molly's ex-fiancé
Kate McLeod (Bad Engagement) — Kelsey's college friend, advertiser extraordinaire, loves purple and Hermione Granger
Jaime Huntingon (Bad Engagement) — vet, does excellent man-bun
Heidi Greene (Bad Bridesmaid) — science, organization, and *Twilight* nerd
Brad Huntington (Bad Bridesmaid) — travel junkie, dreamy hazel eyes, hidden sweet side
Ben Bradford (Bad Swipe) — quiet, brooding, had a thing for golden retrievers

Stef McKay (Bad Swipe) — lab assistant, dog lover, klutzy to the extreme
Tammy Huntington (Bad Girlfriend) — allergic to relationships
Fletcher King (Bad Girlfriend) — has a thing for smart, sassy women

ADDITIONAL CHARACTERS:

George O'Keith — Jordan's dad
Hunter O'Keith — Jordan's nephew
Bridget McGregor — Colin's mom
Lena McGregor — Colin's sister
Bobby Donovan — Heather's half and Trix's full brother
Frances and Sugar Delgado — Sera's parents
Devon Scott — Kels and Bas's brother
Becca Scott — Kels and Bas's sister in law
Fred — the bestest golden retriever in the world
Sir Fuzzy McFeatherston aka The Fuzz — Jaime and Kate's pet rooster

One

Cora

Cheetos were really the best thing on the planet.

Okay, maybe not the *best* thing.

Because she *could* list a few things that were better than the faux cheese crunchy deliciousness—those being her mom's chocolate pecan pie, the croissants from Molly's in her new hometown (San Francisco had a lot of perks compared to the small suburban city that she had grown up in, not the least of which were the delicious treats from her favorite bakery), and sitting at home in her fuzziest socks while watching the Hallmark channel on repeat.

Those were all better than Cheetos.

But truly, they were all a close second. At that moment anyway.

Which was mostly because she had her bag of chips propped on the couch next to her, her orange powder-covered fingers—on her left hand, always, since the right hand was reserved for the remote so she could pause for a heartfelt sigh at all the perfect parts. And to rewind and watch them again.

And to sigh again.

She also had a box with baked goods on her coffee table—minus one croissant because she couldn't wait until the morning—and hell, why should she? It was Friday night. She was single since her brothers had decided to chase off the last man she'd dated.

Truthfully, she couldn't complain too much.

Six brothers equaled a lot of testosterone, and when they got it in their heads that she needed protecting, it was nearly impossible to get them to stop.

They were dogs to a bone.

Mostly because they had been protecting her almost her whole life.

Five. She'd been five years old when her dad died. The youngest. The baby. The long-awaited girl after *all* those boys. She needed to be protected. Coddled. Looked out for. It was sweet but stifling. Loving but overbearing. Coming from a genuine place but sometimes so absolutely infuriating that she wanted to tear her hair out.

Her older brothers had made it their full-time jobs—complete with benefits, plenty of PTO, and 401k plans—to watch over her.

Her dad had ingrained it in them.

Her dad, whom she loved...but—she sighed—she just wished she had the memories her brothers did, her mom did.

Everything she had was blurry on the edges, more feelings and smells than crystal clear memories.

Being tossed up in the air, flying so high that she felt like she could grab the stars twinkling overhead.

The smell of his skin, his hair.

The feel of his strong arms hugging her tight.

It was enough...and it wasn't *nearly* enough. She wanted what her brothers, her mom had, but knew she would never get it. So, she contented herself with the stories, the fractured memories, and pushed the longing she felt for all that she'd missed out on deep, deep down.

So many people had it worse.

She could suck up her daddy issues, be grateful for her family—even for the big lugs that seemed determined to mess up her love life—and enjoy her Cheetos and Hallmark.

"Exactly, Cor," she whispered to herself. "Cheetos. Croissants. Forests in Vermont where small-town girls find their happy endings with lumberjacks who have thick, bushy beards and plaid shirts that threaten to burst from the sheer size of their biceps."

Pleased with herself—go, new positive Cora!—she hit play on the remote and allowed herself to get wrapped back up in the story.

And God, seriously, those colorful leaves were *gorgeous*.

She was thinking that she really needed to plan a trip to Vermont when there was a knock at her door.

"Ugh," she groaned, wishing she could ignore it. But if it was one of her brothers, they would just let themselves in anyway, and if she wanted to protect her Cheetos from their Hoovering abilities, then she needed to be proactive.

Which meant answering the door.

After stashing the bag of Cheetos behind the pillow.

Sighing, she paused her movie, did her stashing, wiped her Cheeto fingers on the napkin she had draped over her leg for just that purpose, then stood.

A glance through the peephole had her sighing again, this time paired with shaking her head. It was so much worse than her brothers.

It was *him*.

She tugged open the door.

"Rafe," she grumbled, plunking her hands on her hips, "which of them sent you?"

Yeah, she had six brothers, but she might as well have a

seventh because Rafe had hung around Jeremy, Wyatt, and Asher—her eldest three brothers who had all come within three years of each other (her poor mother)—all the way through elementary, middle, and high school and well into adulthood.

Case in point, he just shrugged, barged into her house, and said, like it was absolutely no surprise (and she supposed it wasn't), "All of them."

She muttered an epithet, closed the door he'd just left wide open, and hurried past him, lest he try to steal her croissants.

With six brothers, she'd learned to protect what was really important.

Which was why she grabbed the bag of Cheetos right after she'd safely secured the box of pastries.

He dropped a bag on the floor—right in the middle of her living room—and sank onto the couch, picking up the remote and changing the channel, like he'd visited a hundred times before.

And she supposed he had.

He always seemed to tag along.

To *protect* her.

And yes, she was mentally doing air quotes to go along with that thought, even as she shoved his feet off the coffee table. "What are you doing here?" she growled, snatching the remote back and returning the television to its rightful place—the Hallmark channel.

But she didn't get to rewind the movie back to where she'd left off.

Because Rafe shrugged his bulky shoulders, nodded at the bag, and said—

"I'm moving in."

Two

Rafe

He plunked his feet back on the table, snagged the pale blue pastry box before Cora could complain.

She jerked forward like she was going to snatch it from him, but because she already held the bag of Cheetos and the remote, her attempts to keep her treats to herself were thwarted.

He opened the lid, snagged a croissant that was drizzled heavily with chocolate, and jammed a huge bite into his mouth.

Mostly because he knew that she'd do her level best to snatch it back.

But the blue box was from Molly's.

And he didn't pass up a chance for Molly's.

Her noise of outrage chased his second bite, and then she was tucking the bag of chips behind her, reaching for the box, and plunking it onto the side table at her end of the couch.

"You never did like to share," he teased.

She glared. "You never did like to ask before you took my things."

God, she was cute with her glary eyes, her fluffy slippers, and her ratty robe printed with unicorns that he'd seen her wear at least a hundred times over the years. "With six siblings, you're used to that."

More glaring. This one not deemed to be paired with a reply.

Or rather, the reply was that she pushed the box of pastries farther away from him, held her Cheetos tighter to her chest, and then turned the volume up on her movie.

"How's work?" he asked.

A shrug. The volume clicked up.

That sent his spidey sense tingling. Her boss was an asshole.

He didn't know why she'd left Robotech and transitioned to the startup the previous year, but he knew she wasn't happy in her new position.

Not that she said anything.

Well, *that* was why his spidey senses were tingling.

Cora was a woman who didn't limit her words. She spoke and did it a lot, and he had to admit that as entertaining as he often found her, sometimes his mind drifted a bit...especially when she talked about work.

Which she wasn't doing.

Hadn't been doing.

For several months now.

And she was home on a Friday night, wearing her ratty robe, eating Cheetos, and watching shitty Hallmark movies.

Why was that?

Why *was* that?

She sighed, and he glanced over at her. But she wasn't looking at him. In fact, her gaze was glued to the TV, and he watched her watch that lame movie.

Until she sighed again.

It wasn't Cheeto-related (she was chowing down on those like it was her fucking job to get every last crumb out of the bag). It also wasn't croissant-related (she still had ten in the box, and yes, he'd counted...as he'd shoved one in his mouth). He didn't think it was related to him barging into her living room (even if she was annoyed, she'd had years of practice with him and her brothers doing it). She'd had years of being barged in on and because Cora was a practical woman, he just didn't see her getting exceptionally frustrated with something that wasn't going to change.

So, what else was it?

Another sigh.

"What's up, baby doll?" he asked.

Bouncing curls as she turned her head in his direction. "You trying to chit-chat and distract me isn't going to work," she said. "I've got all my treats securely protected." A shrug. "Or securely in my belly," she added.

With that, she tipped the bag up to her mouth, dumping the dredges of the Cheetos in.

Rafe grinned. He'd never seen this woman eat a salad—or not one without a slab of steak sitting beside it, anyway—and he loved that she wasn't shy about downing snacks. He *could* have done with her sharing those snacks more willingly, especially when they involved Molly's, but he liked that she wouldn't ever be the kind of woman to pick at her food just because he was in the same room as her.

Hell, she'd eaten him under the table plenty of times before.

"I'm not trying to distract you," he began.

But didn't get any further, mostly because she snorted and turned back to the TV.

The volume went up again.

She returned to ignoring him.

And the sighing continued.

And...he couldn't pinpoint why there was a niggling in his brain. Something was off with her, but he didn't know what.

And he didn't like it.

Rafe wasn't a man who didn't know things. For as long as he could remember, he understood his place in the world, and he got what he wanted—whether it was answers or respect or success. Also, yes, he knew that made him sound like a cocky bastard, but—here, he mentally shrugged—confidence was sometimes more important than actual skill.

So, Cora being off didn't please him. He wanted to know what was going on and he wanted to know right then, especially if it meant that some asshole was responsible for her being off—because between her boss and the assholes she dated, she was surrounded by a plentiful cluster of the fuckers.

It wasn't out of the realm of possibility that someone had wronged her.

So, it wasn't out of the realm of possibility that Rafe would have to get off his ass and make that wrong a right.

Cora was his, and he protected his family, would always protect them—

She sighed.

He reached his limit, snagged the remote from her, and muted the TV.

"Hey!" She lunged, tried to grab the remote back.

Which meant that he tossed it across the room.

It *clunked* against the far wall, and she turned to him, mouth agape for a long moment. "Seriously?" she muttered.

"What's up?" he asked again.

A huff, the couch depressing as she pushed to her feet. "You're unbelievable, you know that, right?"

He grinned. "Yup."

A muscle in her jaw ticked. "And by unbelievable, I mean that you're an ass."

"I *have* an ass." He grinned. "A nice one from what I've been told."

"Christ," she muttered, starting to move past him.

He snagged her arm. She twisted, her eyes hitting his before flicking down to where his fingers circled her wrist. Olive wrapped around mahogany, her skin like silk beneath his own, her bones delicate and fragile and—

Her eyes narrowed.

She yanked her arm free, stomped over to the remote.

"Is this about me moving in?"

"*If* you were moving in," she said as she bent and retrieved the remote, "I would be annoyed, but since you're not..."

She dropped back onto her end of the couch, hit the volume.

"I *am* moving in."

Now she hit mute, turned to face him, and ordered, "Spill."

"Asher thinks—"

She groaned, arm and remote flopping to the couch.

"That you need someone here in case—"

Another groan, this one paired with her other hand reaching into the pastry box and taking out a croissant. She shoved an admirably large bite into her mouth and chewed while keeping her eyes on the television.

"—you run into some trouble or you need—"

Her gaze drifted to his. "In case I need...what?"

She'd led him down a twisting path, and at the end of that winding trail was a thicket of spiky blackberry bushes.

He sighed. "Look," he said. "You know I'm firmly on Team Protect Cora, but I also get that you're a grown-up and need your own space."

She glanced from the box to him. "Oh, *do* you?"

Shit. She had a point there. See what he meant about her and words? She was too damned good at them.

So, he gave her the truth.

"It was Asher or me," he said. "And since I have a job in town for a few weeks—a job I'll be very busy at, which means I won't be here, cramping your Friday night of bad movies and carbs—I figured you'd prefer me."

Cora pressed her lips together, sighed.

"Am I right?"

The volume clicked up.

"Because otherwise I could call Asher and go hole up at a hotel until your brothers come to their senses—or until you get arrested for fratricide."

She made a face.

Or at least that was what he supposed was happening, given he could only see one-half of her expression. But the half he *could* see went all weird and crinkly, and he knew her well enough to know that she was pouting.

Or fuming.

Or raging silently while calling him every single bad name she could think of inside her head.

And since next would come raging vocally, he decided to go for the kill...or rather, the nail in the proverbial coffin that would put this argument to rest.

He pulled out his cell and started dialing.

"What are you doing?"

"Calling Asher."

"You *are* not."

He lifted his brows, held up his cell so she could see the screen...which was filled with Asher's contact info.

All he had to do was hit the green call button.

Now he got to see the face she was making. It was fucking cute.

It did not dissuade him from his quest.

Which she knew.

Because she sighed, grabbed the bakery box, and extended it in his direction. "Since you're staying," she grumbled.

Victory!

Those were so few and far between with Cora that part of him felt like he should fist-pump, but because he didn't want to stomp on that victory that had just been won (and risk losing it), he shut his mouth, snagged a croissant, and settled in.

To watch bad movies.

Tomorrow, he'd work on gaining control of the remote.

THREE

CORA

"And *then,*" Kelsey said, "I told Tanner that if he didn't tie me up right then, I was going to—"

There was a choking noise from the kitchen.

From *Rafe* in the kitchen.

Who'd been—she leaned to the side, glared at the pass-through to the man in the kitchen—drinking out of the milk carton.

Out of the milk carton.

Her organic, hormone-free, very expensive—and very Californian—milk.

Backwash. *All* up in there.

And now milk dripping down his chin.

And wide eyes on that handsome, annoying face.

His gaze hit hers, surprise in the depths of his emerald green eyes, but she merely raised her brows. If he didn't want to be part of Margarita Night, then he shouldn't have moved into her house. Him overhearing Kels's hilarious attempts to reenact their latest co-read (they didn't have a book club because they read far too many books for that, but they did also tend to read the same books at the same time, especially if it was a spicy new release from one of their favorite authors).

Tanner—Kels's hubby—was sexy and exuded confidence, and Cora knew for a fact that he and Kels had a fulfilling sex life, so the idea of him balking slightly because Kels wanted to act out one of those spicy scenes had them all in giggles.

Kate—sweet, kind, and in the cute baby belly stage—giggled at whatever else Kelsey said.

And because Heidi and Stef both began cackling, Cora knew it had been good.

And she'd missed it.

Because of the big, annoying lug in the kitchen.

She narrowed her eyes.

He lifted a brow, took another drink from the milk carton.

"Did I tell you guys about the last guy I dated and the handcuff incident?"

Slowly, the milk carton lowered.

Now both brows were up, and they were paired with fire in his green eyes. Protective instincts prickled.

Right.

This was why she didn't normally talk about the "fairer" sex when her brothers were around (fairer because they were big babies about splinters and eating vegetables and man flus).

Well, in for a penny, in for a pound.

He wanted to move in?

Then he could hear about handcuffs.

"Well," she said, deliberately turning her attention from Rafe and focusing back on her friends, "you know that he wasn't packing, and he didn't know how to use it."

Another choke from the kitchen.

One she ignored this time, deliberately not looking at the interloper in the other room.

"I thought that he might get inspired if we got a little freaky."

Kate grinned.

Kels, Heidi, and Stef cackled again.

"So, I bought these handcuffs, and I had them couriered to his place, along with a key to my front door and a note telling him that I would be waiting in bed naked." She felt her cheeks go hot, was damned glad that her skin didn't show her blush because she was forgetting that this story was embarrassing and she wanted to sound nonplussed, especially in front of Rafe. "Then, because he was really dumb and I didn't think he'd get it, I added a postscript."

"Oh Lord," Heidi said in the way that only a friend who'd known her from all the way back in college could say (that being with equal parts knowing and horror).

"What did it say?" Stef breathed in a tone that said she was a newer friend and as such, didn't know the mess Cora could make of her life.

"It said that I was ready and waiting and expecting to be fucked."

This time the choke was louder.

Kels shrugged. "I mean, you're a woman who knows what you want, so I'm not seeing the problem here."

"Well, the problem is that he came over and started to use the handcuffs."

"Okaaay," Kate began.

"But he forgot the key."

Stef frowned but didn't say anything, probably wondering what the big deal was.

"And he tightened them too much."

That frown deepened.

"Which meant that my hands started falling asleep—"

Raised brows.

"And he panicked and instead of just going back to his place and getting the key like a normal person because it wasn't an emergency, he whipped out his cell and called 9-1-1 and—"

"Oh, God," Kate began.

Cora nodded. "Right."

"Please, tell me that this isn't going where I think it's going."

"You mean to firefighters busting my lock on the front door because Kenny was too panicked to answer it? Or maybe you might be wondering if the sexy men in navy blue saw me in my full, naked glory?"

"Um, for the record," Stef said softly, "I'm wondering about both."

"I already *know* it's both," Heidi announced.

"Oh, Cora," Kate murmured.

"Right," she said. "So, there's a little gem for you." She cleared her throat, added brusquely, shifting so she couldn't see the kitchen, couldn't see *Rafe* in the kitchen (Rafe, who was emanating very unhappy vibes. Rafe, who was making her feel like she was ready for the floor to open up and let her fall through in order to avoid those unhappy vibes...and she could only hope that the unhappy vibes wouldn't transform into him telling her brothers about the handcuff incident...and also, this just in, she was an idiot because she'd thought that this would teach Rafe a lesson, but really, all it was going to do was rile his protective side, make it difficult to look him in the eye, and reinforce that she always opened her mouth far too soon and way before she thought things out), "Anyway. My brothers might have run him off, but, truthfully, I wasn't sad to have an excuse to wave goodbye."

"Yeah," Kate said, quipping in a way that was totally not Kate, but also totally awesome, "that's bound to happen when a sexy fire brigade sees your hoo-ha."

Cora glanced at Heidi.

Heidi's lips twitched. Then she glanced at Stef. *Her* lips twitched.

Then Cora lost the battle, and embarrassment gave way to laughter because laughter was the best medicine, and even though she was hopelessly single and spent her Fridays alone in a ratty robe with Cheetos and croissants, she still had her friends and margarita nights and Thursday dinners and…a lovable, albeit annoying septuple of men who cared about her.

Even if they were cock-blocks.

Even if one of them was currently pondering investing in chastity belts.

"Hoo-ha is never allowed to pass through your gorgeous lips again, m'kay?" she teased, when she'd managed to get herself together.

"As long as you know that you're not allowed to play with handcuffs again," Kate countered.

Sassily.

Apparently, pregnancy hormones brought the sass.

Cora liked it.

Even though it was Sass Lite. Even though she knew it was less baby-related and more because her friend had found a partner who'd given her the confidence to be herself. Not that Kate hadn't been herself…it was just that Kate had been hurt and there had always been something a bit fragile and vulnerable about her.

That meant they'd all been careful with her, and she'd been careful, too.

This wasn't careful.

This was confidence and teasing and a woman comfortable in her own skin.

And Cora *really* liked that.

Which was why she nodded and then because she was no stranger to sass herself, she added, "At least not without a skeleton key within reach."

Stef hooted.

Heidi grinned. "Why do I think that you've bought a half dozen of those keys and have them stashed around the house?"

Cora waggled her brows. "Because you've known me for a solid decade?"

More laughter, and then Cora reached for the blender that was sitting on the table, virgin margaritas (for camaraderie with the baby-making machine) mostly depleted. She made her way into the kitchen, half expecting Rafe to still be standing there with disapproval on his face, the contaminated milk carton in his hand.

But he wasn't in sight, and the carton of milk was back in the fridge where it belonged (she knew because she checked).

And she wasn't disappointed that he'd gone.

She was happy that he was giving her privacy.

Well, either that or he was calling her brothers and sending an SOS to the entire Hutchins clan to descend upon their sister who'd been corrupted by romance novels and mildly kinky sex.

Maybe he was doing that along with buying stock in chastity belt companies.

Next thing she knew, she'd get all *Robin Hood: Men in Tights* up in there.

"Fun," she whispered as she dumped ice and margarita mix into the blender. Her life was so freaking fun.

"We all know that Jaime was ready with those restraints," Heidi teased, referencing Kate's hubby's profession—as a vet, he'd had to restrain a fair number of tough customers. "And Tanner balked but followed through."

Cora bit back a laugh, doubly so when Kels's cheeks went bright pink.

"So, what about Ben?" Heidi asked. "What did he think of our last book?"

It was Stef's turn for pink cheeks.

And for eyes darting away, even as a satisfied smile creased her expression. "Let's just say that Ben was thoroughly inspired."

They cackled. There was no other word for it.

And Cora joined in.

Because it was a cackle-worthy moment, and because she was so fucking happy for her friends to have found the people they loved and just because she was single didn't mean that she wasn't thrilled they had that.

It was just...

She was lonely.

FOUR

RAFE

Handcuffs.

Fuck.

He really shouldn't be thinking about handcuffs and Cora.

Hell, just the two words near each other in a thought should send his gut churning, bile burning the back of his throat.

Instead, he felt…weird.

The same weird he'd felt when he'd suggested that he stay in Cora's spare room. The same weird that he'd felt when he'd watched her creep of a high school boyfriend grab her ass before they'd left for prom.

Protective.

But not simply that.

And *that* was when he cut the thought off in its tracks. Danger led down that path, and as an honorary member of the Hutchins family (and a dishonored member of his *own* family), he valued his place, wouldn't do anything to fuck it up.

Sighing, he cracked the door, listening for any sound of

cackling.

The women had quieted down earlier, but after the handcuff speak, he wasn't taking any more chances.

Yes, he'd hidden.

No, he wasn't ashamed of that.

Probably, he should have informed Cora's brothers of the handcuff incident, but since he'd been part of the "intervention" (a.k.a. the intimidation) to scare off the asshole who was a bigger asshole than Rafe had previously thought, he figured that letting sleeping dogs lie in this case was better for everyone.

Because they really didn't need to revisit the fact that she had handcuffs, was apparently a little kinky—

Sweet Christ.

He cleared his throat.

Her brothers didn't need to know that apparently, the entirety of the local fire department had seen her naked.

After a few minutes of not hearing any cackling or the reverberations of any bad reality TV, he crept into the hall and—

"*Oof!*"

Fuck, that was a tackle.

He stumbled back a couple of steps, his lower back ramming into the doorknob as a lush, warm body threatened to take him to his knees.

"Shit!" Cora hissed, losing her balance and falling into him harder.

The door slammed back into the wall with a crash. His hands closed around her, holding her tight, catching her against him when she would have fallen to the floor.

She smelled spicy, like cinnamon and apples.

She *felt*...

Curves. Soft. *Woman*.

Shit.

He dropped his hands.

Then immediately had to grab her again when she stumbled

and would have hit the hardwood floor.

He hit it instead, his ass plunking down onto the floor, a sharp burst of pain radiating up his spine. She dropped onto his thighs, her breasts hit his chest, but he didn't let her go this time, even though she was basically straddling him, and his hands were full of woman.

Of Cora.

Fuck.

He reacted without thinking, shoving her off him abruptly.

She landed with a pained grunt, and guilt swarmed him. "Shit, Cor," he began, "I'm sorry—"

"It's fine," she said, shoving to her feet.

He reached to help her...and encountered skin.

Bare skin.

His fingers grazed her thigh, silken fabric fluttering over the back of his hand.

He jerked back like he'd been scalded. And maybe he *had* been. Because that skin beneath his palm had been softer than the hem of the short robe she was wearing. Because that touch had been...he could still feel it, his fingers tingling, a bolt of heat shooting south, shooting toward an appendage that shouldn't be in existence when he was around her.

"I'm sorry," he said again, scrambling to his own feet and lurching for the switch by the door. He flicked it on. "Are you...?"

His question stoppered up in the back of his throat.

Because that robe.

That robe.

It was white and shining and...*sheer.*

Hips and ass and when she spun to face him, blinking, probably at the sudden brightness of the overhead light, his gaze wasn't caught on her pretty brown eyes. It was on...

Breasts.

Large, round globes pressing against silk.

Hardened nipples perfectly outlined.

His cock twitched.

Fuck. *Fuck.* He needed to burn out his retinas.

He averted his eyes, swallowed hard, and determinedly focused on the door...and the knob that had wedged itself into the sheetrock behind it.

"Shit," he muttered, tugging it forward and wincing at the puff of dust that emerged.

That was a decent-sized hole.

"Good thing you're in construction," she said. He hadn't heard her approach, hadn't heard her get close to him, and her words made him jump.

And glance down.

Breasts.

Fucking *hell*, she had *breasts.*

"What?" he croaked.

Cora lifted her brows, the edges of her kissable mouth curving up.

Kissable—

Wait, *what?*

She nudged his shoulder with hers, and fucking heaven help him, but her breast brushed against his arm. He was *so* a breast man. He lived to touch and squeeze, to lick, suck, and nibble the delicious globes, but Cora wasn't supposed to have breasts.

And she definitely wasn't supposed to have breasts that he noticed and—

"Did I break you?" she teased. "I *said,* it's a good thing that you're in construction."

She went to bump him again.

He backed away, returning his focus toward the hole, but not before he saw the flash of hurt cross her face.

Fuck.

"Right," she whispered, "I'm going to get my hot chocolate and head to bed."

"You still do that?" he asked, turning to face her, unable to *not* look at her.

Growing up, he'd slept over at her childhood home so many times that he'd begun to understand the ebbs and flows of the Hutchins family. He knew them as well as his own breath, his own preferences and habits.

Cora was a night owl.

God, he couldn't remember how many times he'd made her a cup and they'd sat on the couch in her mom's basement when she couldn't sleep, playing *Mario Kart* or watching some borderline inappropriate movie for her age (think: *Speed* and *Die Hard* when she was eight or nine).

They'd watched or played until her eyes began to droop.

Then he'd swept her tiny body up into his arms, carried her up into bed, and tucked her under the covers more times than he could count.

But she didn't have a little girl's body now.

She was a woman, and he was desperately wishing that was a fact he hadn't noticed.

Her eyebrows lifted nearly to the black silk of her hair wrap, but she just shrugged. "Hot cocoa is still the best drink on the planet."

"Because you still don't sleep well?"

Those brows relaxed, her shoulders rose and fell on a shrug —and fucking hell, her breasts jiggled with the movement.

He skittered back another step, dropped his stare to the ground.

Sweet, sweet baby Jesus.

"I sleep fine."

He watched her feet, watched them turn for the hall. Watched them pause, just on the threshold of the door.

"Goodnight," she whispered.

He stared at the opening long after she'd gone.

Which was why he knew that she hadn't gone down to the

kitchen, that she hadn't gotten her hot chocolate, that she probably wasn't sleeping, even though the house was still and quiet, even though there wasn't one bit of noise from her end of the hall.

And as he stared, he replayed that flash of hurt, the soft goodnight, over and over.

He replayed it long after the sound of her footsteps disappeared, long after he should have gone to sleep.

He replayed it so long that eventually he found himself listening to the sound of his own footsteps descending the stairs, padding across the floor into the kitchen. The clink of the mug, the beep of the microwave.

The creak of the cabinets as he searched for the good chocolate, because he knew she had to have some stashed somewhere.

Cora without chocolate was...unfathomable.

And there it was. A large stack of expensive bars. He opened one, broke up half into small chunks, and dropped them into the warm milk, microwaving it again to get it all to melt.

A stir. A dollop of marshmallow cream. A heavy dose of caramel syrup. A vigorous stir. Plenty of whipped cream and chocolate syrup and more caramel syrup on top.

Her special comfort hot chocolate. From him. From the recipe *he'd* created for her.

Then he was walking up the stairs.

Then he was walking down the hall, carrying the steaming mug with its whipped cream melting on top.

Carrying it to Cora's room.

Knocking on the door.

Waiting, his heart hammering against his ribs, knowing that something had changed and yet understanding that *nothing* had.

No answer.

He knocked again, beginning to wonder if perhaps he'd misjudged the quiet, misconstrued the silence and the direction of her footsteps.

Maybe she'd fallen asleep.

Maybe she'd already gotten the—

The door swung open.

Cora stood there in her robe, her skin glistening like she'd been in the bath, or maybe like she'd just been thoroughly fucked—and fucking hell, that thought shouldn't be passing through his mind, it *should not* be in his mind at all. Beautiful. Grown-up. Tempting.

But her eyes were cautious.

And that reminded him why he was standing outside her door in the middle of the night.

"Here," he blurted, shoving the mug at her, the hot chocolate nearly spilling over the rim. "To help you sleep."

Then he spun on his heel, ran—yes, *ran*—down the hall and into the spare room, closing the door firmly.

Probably more firmly than he should have.

But the wood between them was necessary.

The fierce *click* also required.

To remind himself who he was. Who *she* was.

He turned off the lights, slid into bed, tugging the covers over himself, even though he was sweating, even though part of him was burning up inside.

With need.

For Cora.

For his best friends' sister.

Who had lush curves, a set of breasts that a man dreamed of, an ass that should have been illegal. His dick twitched, and he groaned, rolling to the side and punching the pillows, trying desperately to forget, to get comfortable.

And knowing that he was fucked.

Because as the hours passed and he finally began to drift off to sleep, all he could think of was what her skin would taste like.

Fucked.

So. Totally. Fucked.

Five

Cora

She held the mug of hot chocolate, the scent of cocoa and whipped cream drifting up to her nose, making her mouth water.

But it was a distant response of her taste buds.

Because...Rafe.

Because of the flash of awareness in his eyes. Of *heat.* Before he'd spun on a heel and took off for his room—no, for the *spare* room, she needed to remember this was her house, her life, her *flipping* room.

"You're losing your mind, Cor," she whispered, turning slowly and closing her door.

She moved to her bed, her robe still sticking to her tub-damp skin, her body overheated from soaking, sleep just curling on the edges of her mind. She'd been drying off, debating between starting the newest book she and her friends were reading together, knowing that could either go really bad or really good depending on how good the book was.

Either she'd be asleep in minutes, or she'd be up until dawn, hiding under the blankets and whispering, "Just one more chapter," to herself and her Kindle.

But the hot chocolate was a surefire sleep technique. That paired with a shoot-em'up was guaranteed to have her out in less than an hour.

The hot cocoa would fill her belly, coat her taste buds, and when she pulled herself out of bed to brush her teeth—because oral hygiene was important, even for insomniacs like herself—she would clean her choppers while she was half-asleep before she stumbled back to her cozy mattress, cuddled beneath the soft blankies, listened to the white noise of explosions and gunfire, and passed out.

And Rafe had given it to her.

With heat in his eyes.

"What the fuck?" she said, or rather kept whispering, moving to the bed, trying to solve the puzzle that was Rafe, but knowing that she wouldn't, knowing that instead she just needed to drink her cocoa and watch her movie and let sleep take her under.

So, she drank her hot chocolate.

She watched Bruce Willis yippee-ki-yay.

And eventually, she stumbled to the bathroom, cleaned her teeth, stumbled back to bed.

And...sleep took her under.

Light was streaming through the windows when she woke, and she groaned as she rolled over, totally unready to face the day.

She hated mornings.

Hated getting out of bed when it meant that she had to start the day.

Luckily, it was Sunday, so she could afford to be lazy for just a bit longer.

Sighing, she tugged the covers up, eyes hitting on the mug—empty because Rafe could make a mean hot chocolate—sitting on her nightstand.

And she was brought back to all the weird from the night before.

The flash of horror in his gaze when he'd accidentally touched her.

God, the man made her feel like a hideous monster.

She knew he was used to seeing her as a little sister, but his reaction was more than a bit ridiculous. She was an adult woman, for God's sake, had been one for the last almost twelve years. Hell, the last time she'd seen her ob-gyn for her yearly torture of speculum and breast exams, she'd been told that her eggs were getting old.

At thirty.

And Rafe was thirty-six.

Jeremy, Wyatt, Asher, Eli, Rowan, Rome...and her.

Jeremy and Wyatt were twins, both had would turn thirty-seven shortly. Asher was thirty-six because, for some godforsaken reason, her parents had decided to try for a third when the twins were only a few months old. Her mom always said she was too sleep-deprived to know better, but she said it in that dreamy way that she always did when talking about her family.

Edy Hutchins was made for home and hearth. Her veins should have been filled with Christmas cookies and the ability to get stains out of sports uniforms.

And...she'd worked her ass off.

Jeremy, Wyatt, Asher, Eli, then surprise! Another set of twins—Rowan and Rome. Six boys under six...and then Cora.

And then...her dad gone.

Probably because of the stress of taking care of seven kids under seven...either that or having superhuman sperm.

"Gross," she whispered, shuddering as she shook that thought out of her head.

Sperm and parents.

Two things she shouldn't *ever* think about.

Sighing again—and God, wasn't this like her teenage years, sighing and shuddering and feeling a bit gross and worthless—she tossed back the covers and moved to the shower. Cleaning her body, not her hair because she seriously did *not* have the time or energy to deal with her hair today, then getting on with her normal Sunday routine.

Moisturizing—hair and body. Touching up her toenail polish, organizing her work outfits for the week.

Black pants and a coral top.

Black pants and a cream blouse with a cute, slouchy bow at the top.

Black pants and a turquoise body suit, topped with her awesome gray plaid jacket.

Black pants—

Sensing a theme here?

Except, she pulled out a surprise on Friday. Because it was Casual Friday at work and that meant she would be wearing black *jeans.*

Go her.

She paired those with a floral button-down, swirls of purple and pink alluding to roses and pansies.

Then she moved on to underwear and bras and shoes.

Because she *really* hated mornings, and though she'd been able to make her own schedule at her previous job with Robotech, her new boss was a stickler. Early to the office, late to leave. Extra hours and emails on the weekends and hustling, hustling, *hustling.*

Which she could appreciate because they were trying to get the company off the ground.

She was willing to put her sweat equity into something great, so long as there was a light at the end of the tunnel, a marker they were moving toward, a finish line to cross.

The only thing was...she'd been wondering if the company was really great.

If there would ever be a finish line, or if that line would keep moving forward, never to be crossed.

She sort of thought that she knew already, the certainty of wrongness having sunk deep into her bones, making it settle there like a second layer of marrow. The company wasn't great—or at least, not great for *her*. And paired with the control her boss wanted to exert over everyone and everything, the micromanaging of every single project that she worked on and was shaded as just making sure everything was "perfect" because it needed to be "perfect" in order for Voldcom to succeed and...she was exhausted.

Too many hours.

Too little freedom.

Too...much thinking for her free day.

She straightened the final pair of shoes for the week then stood up, stifling another sigh because she wasn't going to go full teenager on her free day.

Then she grabbed the mug from her nightstand and left her room.

The house was quiet. Empty.

The door to Rafe's room—to *her* spare room—was closed, but she knew he wasn't inside.

She had inner brother sense, an inner brother detector—and that included Rafe, because God knew he'd been around so much that he fit firmly in that category. Even if...he *was* pretty, and she could appreciate it.

Like a fine art painting.

Gorgeous. Yes. Untouchable. Also, yes. A little off-putting and too fancy-dancy for her.

No.

She liked fancy.
She *liked* untouchable.
She liked Rafe. Had liked him her whole life.
It was just better when she pretended that she didn't.
For everyone.

Six

Rafe

His eyes flashed open, sleep falling away in an instant.

He focused on the room—on the darkness flowing through the windows of Cora's house—and tried to pinpoint what had woken him up.

He snagged his phone, saw it was a quarter to five.

He had to be at the job site in an hour and a half, but his alarm wasn't set to go off for another thirty minutes. Mostly because he was a roll out of bed and go kind of man. Clean clothes, brush his teeth, tumbler of coffee, and call it good.

Showers at the end of the day.

Because by then he would be covered in muck and grime, with sawdust and sheetrock powder. The nature of being a contractor, even for big industrial projects he was supposed to be just overseeing—which, of course, wasn't *exactly* true. He wasn't the kind of man who just oversaw. He liked to get his hands into things, to get dirty, to feel and hold and touch and *know* that everything was put together properly.

Even if it was just putting together an estimate.

He wanted to see the area he would be working in, to just be in it, to feel the concrete beneath his feet, see the walls and judge the plumbness for himself, to breathe in the space and—

There was a noise from downstairs.

And he abruptly remembered that he'd been woken before his alarm.

Narrowing his eyes, he tossed back the blanket and stood, yanking on a pair of sweats and grabbing his phone. He shoved it into his pocket and crept toward the door, tugging it open, glad that he'd oiled the hinges throughout her house the previous day while she'd been bingeing some reality TV show that had nearly given him hives.

A murmur from the first floor had him going stiff.

He knew it couldn't be Cora.

His Cora didn't roll out of bed until at least nine. Plus—he glanced back in the hall, saw that her door was closed—she was most definitely asleep.

Which meant there was someone in the house.

His instincts prickled, and he softly padded down the stairs, phone out and ready to call 9-1-1, wishing that he'd brought his baseball bat along with him.

Lights in the kitchen had him frowning.

He turned the corner, moving into the space, and his frown deepened.

"What the fuck?"

Cora was there—full makeup on, completely dressed in a shirt that was some weird shade of pink with black pants and heels...and sitting at her computer, earbuds in place.

She glanced up at him, her brows drawn together.

She had glasses on.

They were cute as fuck, but her expression beneath them, or rather, her eyes beneath the lenses...they weren't cute at all.

They blazed with irritation.

She glared at him, mouthed, "What. *The.* Fuck?"

Then turned back to her computer, fingers flying on the keyboard, said, "No, Robert, I understand. I've reworked the 2.0 campaign and it's ready to be—"

Her shoulders went stiff.

"I'm—"

Stiffer still.

"I went over and revised that, too—"

Then those shoulders slumped.

A tendril of rage coiled in his stomach, he stepped forward, prepared to yank out the earbud and hang up on the asshole who was railing at her on the other end of the line.

"I—"

Another pause, this time paired with her whipping around and glaring at him again. A sharp shake of her head.

At him.

And that shake worked. He halted in his tracks.

And he watched as she navigated the conversation, as the glare transformed into frustration and then into defeat. Watched as the light faded fully from her eyes, as she focused on a point over his shoulder and continued the conversation.

"Right, Dale. I'll redo it." Her lids slid closed. "Yup. Of course." Her lips turned up at the corners, shifting into a fake smile that *Dale* couldn't see—and one that Rafe fucking hated. "Of course"—her eyes opened, and she glanced at her wrist—"I'll be there in thirty."

Thirty.

Rafe's gaze flicked to the microwave. It was now five to five, and she was going to be in the office in thirty minutes?

That made no sense. Or at least, it didn't fit in with what he knew about Cora.

She did *not* function in the morning.

She did *not* get up early.

She'd...grown up.

And that was...good? Working hard was important. Rising to the occasion even more so.

Except, what wasn't good was the expression on her face, the defeat in her eyes, the long, quiet sigh as she rubbed her forehead.

Her shoulders slumping.

He *really* didn't like that.

She closed her computer, pushed back her chair. Then she was moving to the coffee pot, was pouring herself a tumbler.

"Coffee?" she asked after she'd screwed on the lid.

He blinked. "What?"

"You want a coffee?" she asked, slowly, like he was an idiot.

And maybe he was staring at her like he was. "Yeah," he said, when she waved the half-full pot at him, the scalding liquid inside sloshing around. If only to get her to stop waving it around like she was about to give herself a third-degree burn.

She grabbed another to-go cup, filled it up. "Still like it black?"

"Yeah, Cor. Thanks."

A nod, and then the top was on, and she was carrying it to him, her heels clicking on the hardwood floor. "Here."

"Thanks," he said again.

Another nod.

Then she turned back to the table, tucking the laptop into a black leather satchel that was lying on the table. Another brusque movement had her jacket off her chair, then her arms shoving inside it.

"Cor?"

Her eyes hit his, and there was a cold quality, a lifelessness in those chocolate depths that he really fucking hated.

"You okay?"

Her lips turned up, forcing their shape into that fake smile, one he fucking hated even more, seeing it a second time. "I'm great," she said. "There are cinnamon French toast Eggos in the freezer, Jif in the pantry."

His heart squeezed.

She remembered what he liked for breakfast.

And she had it, even though he'd shown up without warning on Friday, bag in hand, even though she hadn't been happy about him invading.

"Cora," he began. "You didn't have—"

A shake of her head. "I was out. I grabbed some stuff. End of story." She turned for the door. "It's not a big deal."

"Careful," he said gently, "your Edy is showing."

Edy was...amazing. Thoughtful and maternal and caring for others without a second's hesitation. It was instinctual.

And it was Cora, too.

She turned back, her smile softening.

Then shook her head again. "Bye, Rafe."

"You hate it."

He spun, turned to see Teresa, hard hat in place, clipboard in hand, heavy construction boots on her feet that looked way too large for a woman who was all of five foot three inches tall.

But she had freakishly large feet.

Kind of like a hobbit.

Minus the hairy toes.

At least, that was what he figured.

He hadn't seen Teresa's toes, so who knew what she was hiding beneath those giant boots?

"Do you have hairy toes?"

She frowned, her chin jerking back. "What?"

Inappropriate.

He shouldn't be thinking about any part of Teresa, toes or

not. She was his colleague, his project manager, his righthand woman.

And he wanted to keep her there.

Hell, he wanted her to become his partner.

So, step one of that probably shouldn't be asking her about her toes. Step *two* of that definitely shouldn't be asking her about her *hairy toes*. Step three of that—

Shouldn't be blurting out what he blurted out.

"I hate it."

He did. The space. The work that had been completed so far. The whole feel of everything. It was all…wrong.

Teresa had busted her ass on getting the pieces in place before he'd come in to finish them off, and the work had been done properly, cleanly. The space was impeccable.

And…it was all wrong.

She sighed, slapped her clipboard against her thigh.

"I'm—"

He didn't finish the sorry.

Mostly because, as one did—or at least, as *Teresa* did—she was one step ahead of him. "I've already revised the plans," she said, slapping that clipboard to his chest.

He glanced down at the clipboard, at the paper held to the top of the stack.

Floor plans.

His eyes flicked from the page to the space, from the ideas that he knew he would have come up with eventually—eventually, because Teresa had always been smarter than him and much faster than him, and he would have come up with this, but it wouldn't have happened quickly.

And it would have taken a lot of beer, a significant amount of cursing, and then some additional help from Teresa to get to this point.

"This is good," he said.

She grinned.

"Like really good."

Her grin widened.

"Except"—he grabbed a pencil from his pocket, began sketching—"we need to move this wall so that the egress is clear and—"

"*Yes*," she said, snatching both pencil and clipboard from him. "And if we move that wall, then we've freed up space for this bank of offices and can squeeze in another bathroom."

He lifted his brows. "*Another* bathroom? How many can this place possibly need?"

"Have you ever waited in a line ten deep just to use the toilet?"

Rafe shook his head.

"Then you don't know that there really can never be too many bathrooms." She snagged a pen from his pocket, clicked the end, then outlined the square she'd just drawn—this time in pen, as though the non-erasable ink would make it come to fruition.

And it would, he supposed.

Because what Teresa wanted, Teresa got.

He rinsed the last glass and set it carefully in the dishwasher. Then he turned to Mrs. Hutchins, offering, "Can I make you a cup of coffee?"

Wyatt and Jer were in the family room, a hockey game playing in the background, Wyatt chattering about a new girl he was seeing, while Jer was mostly taking the opportunity to give him shit.

But he'd just gotten a free dinner from Mrs. Hutchins.

He needed to make sure he pulled his weight.

And, truthfully, he didn't mind helping wash up. Edy was funny and, for all intents and purposes, had been his mom. He could show that he was grateful for her support over the years by washing a few dishes.

Easy enough.

"You know you don't have to do this," Mrs. Hutchins said, reaching into the cupboard over her head and going up on tiptoe, trying to grab a mug.

"I got it," he told her, snagging enough mugs for everyone, "and do what?" He nudged her lightly with his elbow. "Help my favorite woman wash some dishes after she cooked us a delicious meal?"

"No, honey," she said, something like sadness crossing her face.

"Make you a cup of coffee?"

"Not that either." A pat to his shoulder. "I just—"

"Is there any pie left?" Jer asked, striding into the kitchen. "Oh, coffee? Want me to pour you a mug, Mom?"

"Rafe's got it, honey."

Jer's eyes connected with his, nodded approvingly.

Thanking him for taking care of his mom.

"Good." Jer nodded to the hall. "It's intermission, do you still want me to hang that picture in the hall?"

"Yes, baby." Mrs. Hutchins pressed a kiss to Jer's cheek. "If you have time. Otherwise, I can do—"

"I got it," Jer said firmly. "When we love people, we take care of them. That's what Dad always said, and that's what we do as Hutchinses."

Edy smiled, patted the cheek she'd kissed. "You're a good son, baby."

Jer grinned, kissed the top of her head. "That's the only kind to be, Mom."

Seven

Cora

Her feet ached—stupid fucking heels that she'd *stupidly* decided to wear on a *stupid* fucking Monday that had started too *fucking* early and had ended stupid *fucking* late.

But her head ached more.

Because Dale...was being Dale.

And he was exhausting. No, *she* was exhausted. Okay, well, he was exhausting, too. It was just...she was done.

So *fucking* done.

But Voldcom was so close, so freaking close, and she wanted to be part of that.

She'd just...send out her resumé and bide her time and—

Deep breaths.

Lots of deep breathing and meditation and non-virgin margaritas and—

She'd extended her hand, reaching for the knob, readying to push open the door when the wooden panel ripped open, and Rafe stood directly in front of her. His expression was absolutely thunderous, and as she stared at him, trying to process the fury, his fingers wrapped around her wrist and yanked her into the house.

"Oof," she grunted, sprawling against his chest, palms feeling...stuff she really shouldn't.

Okay, feeling muscles and man and...

See? Stuff she *shouldn't* feel.

Which he probably knew because the moment they were clear of the door, he dropped his hands from around her wrist and stepped back, fist clenching like touching her skin was akin to picking up a pile of dog shit with his bare hands.

And that made her feel...*other things* she shouldn't.

Clearing her throat, shoving down that *hurt,* she moved past him, dropping her laptop bag on the table, trying not to limp, but knowing she was because her shoes hurt physically more than the emotional hurt of Rafe acting like she had rabies.

Or maybe it was the fury in his eyes, like she'd done something to disappoint him.

Or maybe it didn't matter because she was tired and hungry and tired and—

"What the fuck are you doing?"

Her head dropped back, eyes hitting the ceiling. "Why don't you ask me a real question, Rafe?"

"Why the fuck don't you tell me why you were out of the house before five and now back after eight?" His brows arched into sharp C's. "Because by my calculation, that's a fifteen-hour day."

She huffed, kept walking. "And how do you know that I'm not getting back from a hot date?"

His laugh was sharp. "Because it's not even eight-thirty?"

Asshole.

"Yeah," he said, the words hot in her ear. Damp and warm and sending goose bumps prickling down her nape, "I *am* an asshole." A beat. "But that doesn't mean I'm wrong. I care about you, Cor. I'm *trying* to take care of you."

Fuck.

Now she was so pissed that she was yelling at him out loud instead of in her head.

Even if he *was* an asshole.

Even if he deserved to have her yell at him.

"I don't need someone to take care of me. I'm an adult and—"

"Yeah, you are, and I'm an asshole who doesn't deserve to be one of you—"

She frowned. "Wait, what?"

"But none of that means I'm wrong," he said, stepping closer. The heat of his chest coming very close to her spine, that nearness tugging at the threads of thought from her mind, scrambling and knotting them. "Because I'm *not* wrong, am I?"

Fury sparking to life, she spun on her heel, jabbed a finger in his direction. "What I'm *not* doing is spending another second dealing with your bullshit, and that includes you questioning me about my life and my job and what fucking time I come home from it."

"So, you're admitting that you've just worked fifteen hours."

"Ugh." She threw her hands up, spun on her heel a second time—and sweet Christ, that hurt. "What I'm doing is none of your...*ah!*"

One second, she was stomping away, and the next she was in the air.

Rafe's arms were around her, one at her waist, one behind her shoulders, and then she was colliding with his chest.

She shoved at that chest, his muscles bunching beneath her palms, but she might as well have been trying to push her way through a brick wall for all the good it did her. Then they were moving, or rather, *he* was, carrying her across the kitchen and plunking her onto the counter. "Sit," he growled.

"I'm not a fucking d-*ah-og!*"

She'd barely come to terms with her ass hitting the granite when Rafe backed up.

But he didn't go far, just bent and yanked one shoe and then the other off her feet, chucking them over his shoulder. She heard them collide with the cabinets behind her, one after the other.

"You better not have chipped the paint on my—"

Suddenly, his face was *right* there.

In front of hers, his lips...

She inhaled sharply.

"You're limping," he growled, "because of these dumbass shoes."

"They are *not* dumb," she growled back (because if he could growl, then so could she, dammit!). "They are expensive and sexy as hell. So, you just need to—" She started to slide off the counter, but before she could, he planted a hand on her thigh.

One big broad hand totally encompassing her thigh.

"Limping."

One *word.*

Intense. Sharp.

Sliding down her spine.

"I'm fine."

His hand convulsed. Fingers tightening, his thumb pressing against her inner thigh, sending a bolt of heat skating between her legs.

Another inhale, her lips parting and—

"Fifteen *fucking* hours." More growling.

Her chin came up. She pushed his hand away. "It's my fucking life, and if I want to work *fifteen* freaking hours, then I can."

His eyes sparked with fury, green depths flashing with gold and brown, blazing into hers. His hand returned, and then the other one dropped onto her other thigh. "You'll burn yourself out."

He was right.

Which pissed her off even more.

She *was* burned out. Because she was exhausted and ready to quit and desperate to *not* be working fifteen-hour days.

But she didn't need the overbearing asshole telling her what she was feeling and what she should be doing, and fuck, if she wanted to wear uncomfortable heels, then that was her freaking prerogative, even if they *were* giving her blisters on the backs of her heels and she wasn't sure if her arches would ever recover.

But it was *her* life.

Not Rafe's.

Not her brothers'.

Not Dale's

And, fuck, but it was way past time that she did something about that.

She shoved his hands back. "Get out," she snapped. "*Get. Out.* Get. *The fuck*. Out!"

The anger faded from his expression. "Cora, honey—"

"Get out! Get out! Get—"

He kissed her.

Just slanted his mouth right across hers, parted her lips with a swipe of his tongue, and then he was *kissing* her. Plundering her mouth, kissing her so deeply that she almost felt like the contact was bruising her mouth.

And she didn't care.

The slight bite of pain was overwhelmed by pleasure, by the sheer storm that was Rafe.

Fingers threading into her hair, tilting her head back. His tongue darting deeper, stroking along hers. His hands back on her thighs, spreading them wide. He stepped between her legs, hands sliding to her ass, tugging her forward, tugging her even closer, perching her on the edge of the counter. But she didn't fall. He had her...close.

Oh, God.

He had her close.

He shifted, hands drifting down, coaxing her to wrap her legs around him. And—*oh*—that was good. So good that she didn't hesitate to also wrap her arms around his shoulders, to arch against him, to bring her body flush to his.

To...

He tore his mouth away from hers.

One second, she was dangling in a web of pleasure, her limbs and torso wound tight in the silk, floating weightless and out of her mind. And the next...

That spider was coming close.

That spider was descending, readying to devour her.

That spider...was gone.

Leaving so fast that her feet hit the hardwood with a jar that clinked her teeth together, that her hands scrambled to grip the counter behind her, so she didn't end up on her ass.

The front door opened and closed.

Her lips pulsed.

Her breaths came in rapid gusts.

Her legs shook...so hard that she found herself sinking to the hardwood anyway, sinking slowly but inexorably down to the cold, solid surface.

And she sat there, the pleasure slowly fading, the pain in her feet creeping back in, the fatigue, the mental drain, the...

Tired.

She was so, so tired.

Eight

Rafe

He needed to go jump off a bridge.

Like literally, to put himself out of his misery.

Definitely before Cora told her brothers that he'd accosted her in her kitchen.

I was just trying to take care of her…by shoving my tongue down her throat.

"Fuck," he muttered, getting out of his truck—and yes—*slamming* the door shut. Luckily, he was alone on this stretch of the highway, the streetlamps few and far between on the curving road that followed the coastline of the Pacific, so no one was around to hear him have his hissy fit. "Fuck," he said again. "*Fuck.*"

He gripped his hair, tempted to yank it out by the roots, and forced out a sharp breath.

Cora didn't want him butting into her life, so she sure as shit wasn't going to sic her brothers on him, not when it would bring the full force of the Hutchins clan down on them both.

"Fine," he said, rounding the back of his truck and hopping

up to sit on the side of the bed, feet dropped onto the tire, holding him in place when he felt as though the rest of the world would crumble beneath his feet. "It's all going to be fine," he muttered to himself, staring out to the ocean, not able to see much aside from the occasional white froth of a wave breaking, even with the full moon overhead. Dark and dim.

Kind of like his brain.

He snorted, hands falling to his sides, gripping the edge of the bed of the truck, the cool metal nothing at all like Cora's skin.

Soft like silk.

Her curves lush.

Her mouth hot and sleek, her tongue a heated brand as it tangled with his.

Her moans rolling up the back of her throat, drifting across her lips. He'd swallowed it, absorbed the soft groan, felt it sear itself onto his soul. Onto his cock, his brain coming up with all sorts of pleasurable imaginings of how her lips would feel on the head of his dick, how good that warm, hot tongue would be stroking up and down his shaft, how—

"Fuck," he hissed again, slamming his palm against the metal, the loud reverberation even drowning out the waves.

Or maybe that was his pulse pounding in his ears.

Because he shouldn't be thinking about his cock and Cora, her mouth and how fucking good it had been to have her thighs wrapped around his waist.

For all intents and purposes, she was his sister.

But hell, he had never gotten so hard from a fucking kiss.

Ever.

"Why did it have to be Cora?" he whispered.

He blew out a breath, or maybe it was a sigh, or maybe it was just a fuck-his-life exhalation because he knew why.

Because *he* was fucked.

Rolling his shoulders, he stared up at the lightening sky, his face sticky from the damp ocean air, his eyes burning because he was too fucking old to be sleeping in the back of his pickup truck with nothing for a bed except a couple of balled-up sweatshirts and one thin blanket that he used to protect anything that needed protecting when he was hauling it around—wood, furniture, appliances.

But it didn't protect his back...

And now he was exhausted, sticky from the salt in the air, and his back felt like it had been jabbed with a million needles—and not of the acupuncture variety.

But the sun was coming up, and he needed to get his ass in gear.

Because he needed to work himself into exhaustion so that his brain all but melted, too tired to think about what had gone down with Cora.

See?

Good plan.

Muttering a curse, he pushed up out of the bed, used one of the sweatshirts to wipe off his face, snagged the blanket and folded it, stashing it and the extra sweatshirts in the cab of the truck.

Thankfully, he'd had the sense to commandeer one of the company vehicles for his use while he was in town.

Otherwise, he would have had to get a hotel the night before—

Actually, he *should* have gotten a hotel the night before.

Then he would have skipped the whole needles jabbing into his spine thing.

"Right," he muttered, rolling his shoulders, feeling the breeze from the ocean whip up and tear through his hair, the fog rather than the night sky obscuring the waves now. He stood for a minute, listening and staring at the undulating clouds, the mist gathering in places and spreading thin in others, knowing that this wouldn't be his last visit, that there was something that felt like home here.

That maybe that sense of home was more than the ocean or the winding roads hugging a coastline.

More than redwoods growing tall and strong along the shore, more than the invasive ice plants taking over the dunes.

And he worried that where he felt *most* at home was in the small craftsman Cora owned with the sturdy wooden columns, their bottoms wrapped in stone, on Cora's porch with a rocking chair and pots of cheerful flowers stashed in the corners. Walking through Cora's wide front door. Sitting on Cora's sleek gray couch and knowing that it looked atrocious but was incredibly comfortable. Opening and closing Cora's white cabinets and setting out plates on Cora's stone countertops. Padding across Cora's warm hardwood that he'd installed himself—along with Asher and Wyatt—much to Cora's fury, especially since he'd canceled the flooring contractor she'd hired. Using Cora's spare bathroom with the tile he'd installed. Striding up Cora's stairs, holding on to the handrail he'd screwed in, making certain it was secure so that she would be safe.

He got into his truck, turned on the engine, his head spinning, his throat tight.

Because he wasn't stupid. Because he could sense the theme. Because...he wanted to avoid the truth, *had* to avoid it.

But the truth kept smacking him in the face.

Cora.

Home.

And that was what worried him the most.

"Shit," he muttered, the drill slipping, the screw falling to the floor, the bit digging into the sheetrock surrounding the windows he and Teresa were boarding up.

It was dark—well past quitting time—and he knew that the only reason she'd stayed late was because he was here, doing something they could easily send a crew to do in the morning. This property had closed just before five, and so he was technically the owner (he even had the keys and alarm codes in hand, along with the requisite excitement that came from possessing something in the tens of thousands of square feet, something that would become businesses that real people used or office buildings where real people worked, and knowing that he was responsible for that).

But even with the requisite excitement and being the owner, Rafe understood that he didn't really need to be here boarding up windows.

There hadn't been issues with squatting. There weren't any break-ins or even equipment and tools on-site that someone might try to steal, and he'd already arranged for his security company to watch the buildings—and entire complex—overnight.

They were covered.

He was just...avoiding.

Cora.

He was just *avoiding* Cora.

Right. Simple. Cowardly. And...yup...good times for that.

He held the wood with one hand, snagged another screw from the belt hanging around his hips, and plunked it between his lips. Then grabbed another—because at the rate he was going, he was probably going to lose another half dozen of the pointy metal bastards—and positioned it beneath the drill bit.

This time, he was able to screw a piece of wood into the frame without creating unnecessary holes.

So, he repeated the process—screw beneath bit, screw in wall, screw from belt, screw beneath bit, screw in wa—

"You okay?"

The bit wobbled. The screw dropped.

He steeled himself, lifting his eyebrows in question when he turned his head to meet Teresa's eyes.

She'd finished her windows and was watching him with concern written into the lines of her face. "You okay?" she asked again.

"Yup," he muttered around the screw still held between his lips, turning back to face the wood, thankfully finishing the job without making any additional holes, without dropping any more screws. "Just peachy."

Of course, it was just a bonus that she couldn't really hear him, since he was still all but chewing on the sharp metal fastening.

But it also meant that she came closer, holding the wood on his next window while he screwed, coming close enough to see his expression and probably the turmoil within his brain, making his fingers rubbery, his mind fuzzy, his—

"You're not okay."

He lifted his shoulders. Dropped them. "I'm not okay," he said, telling her the truth—or the safe part of it, anyway—because Teresa could sniff out bullshit with the best of them. And, to add to that, it didn't help that he was a shitty liar. "I'm tired," he added before her concern could swirl to worrisome levels. "I didn't sleep well, and Cora isn't all that thrilled that I'm at her place." He detailed the sex talk and the margarita night with her friends.

Teresa smirked. "Sounds like fun."

"If you want to take a flamethrower to your ears so you don't hear about your best friends' sister talking about bondage during sexy time when she's supposed to be innocent and pure forever—"

Except she hadn't been pure when I'd been sticking my tongue down her throat, had she?

He gritted his teeth, shoved the thought away.

It was made easier because Teresa burst out laughing, straight bending over, holding her belly, laughing as she sputtered, "P-p-pure?" A huff. "And *in-in-innocent?*"

"Teresa," he growled.

She put her hand up, palm out. "N-no," she said, still sputtering, "no, I *can't*. You want a grown-ass woman to be pure and innocent?"

He glared.

"You've totally lost it," she said, "I know that you think of her like a little sister, but come on!" More laughter burst forth.

"I'm not seeing the humor in this."

"You *wouldn't*," she muttered, "seeing as you're a big, protective alpha who can't retain your protective alpha status unless you're rescuing poor, helpless maidens."

His glare didn't abate. "That's not fair," he said. "I've never once stepped on your toes in this job."

Gentle snatching amusement, and she stepped close, bumped her shoulder with his. "No, Rafe, you haven't." She tilted her head from side to side. "Okay, well, you did step in and threaten to shove a pry bar into that one sub's eyeball on the Kowalski job."

"He grabbed your ass when you bent over to measure the baseboard!"

Her lips twitched. "He did." Another bump of her shoulder. "But maybe the pry bar-eye threatening was unnecessary?"

"He grabbed your ass," Rafe gritted, "and couldn't keep his *eyes* off your boobs—"

A pat to his cheek—one of the ones on his face. "Which is why you're a big, proud, protective alpha," she murmured in a singsong voice, "with big, proud, protective alpha *tendencies*."

He hissed out a breath. "Teresa," he warned.

"Big, proud, protective alpha tendencies don't make you bad," she said in a tone that was so consoling, he knew it was purposely aggravating. *Gah.* Women. "It just makes you a big, proud, protective, *annoying* man." She grinned. "And I can say that because I have two annoying, proud, protective brothers *and* an annoying, albeit lovable, proud dad."

Rolling his eyes, he took the battery out of his drill, picked up the screws from the floor, and turned for the exit of the building.

The windows were done.

All that was left was to set the alarm, lock the door, and go home.

To Cora.

He inhaled slowly, silently.

Fucking hell.

"Rafe?"

He narrowed his eyes at the still smiling Teresa.

"What?" he asked gruffly.

"Carbs."

His brows pulled together.

"You're in the doghouse," she said, hitting the button on the alarm panel then holding the door closed so he could lock it. "The best way to get out of that is to invest in carbs—ice cream, baked goods, gourmet chocolates. Pick Cora's favorite and bring it home as a just because." She smirked. "Trust me, it'll be the best thing you can do to remedy your living situation."

"Right," he said, pocketing the keys. "I'll do that."

A nudge, a wave, and they exchanged goodbyes.

Then he was in his truck and on his way to invest in his body weight in carbs.

Because he didn't just have to get out of the doghouse.

He had to buy enough carbs to get Cora to forget about that kiss.

Nine

Cora

Well, maybe she'd scared him off for good.

One kiss from Cora and see how they run!

She blew out a breath, rotated her head from side to side, trying not to think about the fact that Rafe had fled after the kiss, that he hadn't returned the night before—and she knew because she'd barely slept, and most of that sleep had happened on the kitchen floor after she'd sat there in a depressed haze, feeling sorry for herself.

If he'd come across her, he definitely would have ordered her to an actual bed.

That being, *not* the hardwood floor in the kitchen, the only benefit of her makeshift bedroom being the heater vent that had blown warm air along her side, thus ensuring she didn't turn into a human popsicle.

When her stomach had finally rumbled loud enough to shake her out of her haze, she'd grabbed a bag of carrots from the fridge, a jar of peanut butter from the pantry—don't judge her, they were good together—and had gone up to her bedroom (the real one, that was) where she had consumed two-thirds of the peanut butter and the entire bag of baby carrots, listening for him to come home while doing her level best to make certain that her consumption of veggies didn't bring any actual nutritional value.

Or that her consumption's nutritional value had been completely canceled out.

But he hadn't come home.

And she'd left work at a reasonable hour—not because of Rafe and his bossiness. But because she was done. Boundaries needed to be drawn. She needed sleep. She wasn't being productive anyway, and she knew that if she was required to be creative (necessary since Dale had basically shit-canned the entire project and she had to start over), she had to be operating on all cylinders.

Dozing on the kitchen floor wasn't conducive to that.

Staying up watching action movies with the subtitles only, realizing that sound was seriously required when captions read, "intense intensity" (umm, what?) and "gunfire and explosions" (way too tame to explain an entire building turning into ash), also didn't allow for the most restful night's sleep.

Also, she was at the IDGAF point with Dale.

He wanted to fire her?

Fine.

He wouldn't be able to finish the campaign without her.

So, yeah, she'd gone home and ordered pizza (with pineapple because, fuck the haters!) and watched bad TV, and she didn't care if Rafe came back to the house. He could stay away for-*ev*-ah—or until the next family holiday...which would be coming up far too soon for her taste, especially considering that Asher's birthday was two weeks away.

Whatever.

She'd deal. And Rafe would have to as well, just pull up those big boy britches, man up, and shut his flipping mouth.

And keep his tongue to himself.

Plus, she hadn't wanted her space invaded in the first place, so if a kiss scared him off, then good.

She should have done it long ago.

"I should do it to my brothers. Then they'd stay away, too, and wouldn't eat me out of house and home—" Shuddering and processing that as she was stomping around, getting her Cheetos and popcorn and wine, and not really understanding the whirlwind that was her mind until those words actually crossed her lips, she realized what she'd said. Kiss her brothers? "Ew," she muttered. "No. I am *so* not doing that. Definitely *not*. No freak—"

The lock clicked in the front door, screeching in the metal slot, and she froze, glass of wine in one hand, her bag of Cheetos in the other.

Her face was covered in green goop. She had her most unflattering pajamas beneath her unflattering and holey robe, which was fuzzy and cozy, but ratty as hell. And—she turned, saw Rafe walking into her house, bags hung on his wrist—she barely fought the urge to whirl around and run upstairs, to go and hide in her bedroom.

Because of the kiss.

Because she was in the most unflattering clothes she owned, with the most unflattering face mask in the history of all face masks globbed onto her face.

She set her wine down.

Rafe moved into the kitchen, the bags crinkling, and...

Fury filled her.

It began in her toes, sparking and prickling up through the arches of her feet, tingling along her calves, the backs of her knees, her thighs, across her stomach, and up between her breasts. Her words bunched up on her tongue, ready to whip forward, to slash and cut and wound. And her nape prickled, her arms strained, her fingers clenched tight into fists.

The bag of Cheetos crinkled as her hand tightened, but thankfully she didn't have her wine glass in hand or else the stem would have certainly shattered.

Well, there was nothing for it.

A breath, ignoring Rafe as he made his way into the kitchen. She turned back to the counter, forced her hands to relax, lest her Cheetos be reduced to dust, and after tucking her bag of popcorn beneath her arm, she deliberately picked up her refilled glass of wine and started for the family room, intending to walk right by Rafe.

And still ignoring him.

If that wasn't obvious.

Because he was evil and awful and...a really good kisser.

Ugh.

"Cor—"

Nope. Not gonna do it.

She sidestepped his outstretched arm, moved into the family room. Cheetos and wine glass on the coffee table. Remote snatched up and finger poised to hit the play button. Throw pillows plumped and—

A familiar bakery box in front of her face.

Rafe sank onto the coffee table, nudging her wine glass to the side, the chardonnay sloshing up near the rim, almost splashing over the top.

She narrowed her eyes. If he spilled so much as *one* drop, so help her God.

He settled the glass, stashed the wine safely next to her Cheetos.

Fine.

The man could live. For the moment.

He crouched, trying to intercept her gaze. But she wasn't going to let him go there, so she deliberately kept her eyes plastered over his shoulder. At least until the box rattled slightly, cinnamon wafting up to tease her sense of smell.

Cinnamon. A Molly's box with cinnamon seeping out of the cardboard.

He didn't. The man *hadn't.* Seriously, he hadn't bought her an entire coffee cake from Molly's. That was going to go straight to her ass, and she wasn't joking.

She also wasn't going to turn it down.

"Cora," he began.

No, dammit. Stay strong over the glorious scent of cinnamon and a drizzle of cream cheese. Even *if* her mouth was watering, and her stomach was definitely not on the *stay strong* train.

She clicked the play button.

A sigh, then the remote was out of her hand, the pause button pressed, her glorious reality binge paused for the moment.

"It's fine," she said, reaching for the remote. "Apology accepted. We can pretend that never happened. Now let me watch my show."

"I didn't even apologize yet."

"Consider yourself off the hook," she muttered. "I know how much you hate apologizing."

"I don't—"

She glanced up at him, lifted her brows...and that was enough to halt his denial.

"Fine," he muttered. "I don't like apologizing." He dropped the box into her lap. "But I should anyway."

And didn't *that* feel good?

Her kisses made men run *and* apologize. Joy!

"Cor—"

God, why wouldn't this end?

But all her protests and snarky response would just draw this out, so she was just going to grin and bear it and—*okay,* she wasn't going to *grin and bear it,* she was just going to *bear it.*

"I'm sorry," he said. "I shouldn't have done that."

Then...silence.

And she realized that was all he was going to say. Some apology. Shouldn't have done *that.*

"Right. You shouldn't have questioned my work habits considering that I'm a grown woman who can choose how many hours I work and what time I wake up in the morning." She lifted her brows higher, waiting for him to challenge her.

But also...sort of holding her breath, waiting to see if he was going to acknowledge the kiss.

Which felt like more than a kiss. It felt like an undoing, like the moment his lips had touched hers, every single part of her had been undone. Torn apart. Then stitched back together in a way that left her feeling changed in a way she hadn't wanted.

Ever.

There was more silence, tense this time as his emerald eyes locked onto hers. Then he said gently, "I worry about you."

Not acknowledging it.

Right.

That wasn't unexpected.

It also shouldn't hurt.

But if they weren't acknowledging things, she could wrap that pain right up in there with the kiss. Pretend it never happened. Be as good as new.

Her chin came up. "But I'm a grown woman, and I can choose how much I work." A beat. "And sleep."

A muscle began to tick in his jaw, making her confidence begin to trickle back in.

Goodbye, pain.

Hello, Cora.

She was back, bitches, and she was going to win this fucking conversation. *If* winning conversations was a thing...and dammit, yes, winning conversations was a thing. Hell, it was an *important* thing, especially with an annoying man who wanted to interject himself into her life. The good news was that she was on the precipice of winning *this* conversation because they were on the precipice of acknowledging The Kiss, and heaven forbid Rafe do *that*. Not when he was trying to get a gold medal in pretending it hadn't happened.

And know what?

She'd take that win, any freaking day of the week.

"Right?" she pressed.

That muscle continued to tick.

His eyes held hers; the air between them crackled.

"Yes," he said finally. "I overstepped, and it won't happen again."

Victory!

She was ready to dig out her pom-poms from somewhere deep in her closet and do a cheer. She was sure she could *dig* out some two-four-six-eight-who-do-I-appreciate from the recesses of her mind.

But she could be gracious.

Out loud anyway.

"Thank you." She snagged the remote again, started to hit the play button, then hesitated. "You know what would really make your apology all that much better?"

His lips pressed flat, amusement nowhere present on his face.

Except in the corners of his eyes, trickling into those emerald depths, warming and glimmering and—

He reached into his pocket, pulled out a plastic-wrapped fork. "This?"

Her heart did a pitter-patter.

Then she shoved it down, plastered a smile on her face...and snatched the fork. Yup, snatched it. Because she had an evening of Cheetos and coffee cake, wine, and reality TV, and she was going to dive right into it.

Even if her heart did another pitter-patter when he sank onto the opposite edge of the couch.

But that pitter-patter was squashed in a second when he pulled out a second fork.

Ten

Rafe

If looks could kill, he would have been six feet under when he tugged the second plastic-wrapped fork from his pocket.

But even though her brown eyes filled with irritation, and her shoulders rose and fell on a loud huff (one that nearly overshadowed the drama of the truly awful—albeit addicting—show that was blaring from the TV), she still put the box between them so he could dig into the coffee cake, too.

He should have apologized, gone upstairs.

Left her to her sugar and wine and bad TV and put some much-needed distance between them.

Except...he couldn't.

He was glued to the show, couldn't peel himself away from the coffee cake—

Lies.

Well, both of those were true.

But the lie was that he was tiptoeing around the biggest reason he'd stayed.

Cora.

Because he was glued to her, couldn't pull himself away from her riot of brown curls, the slender curve of her nape and shoulders, the way her breasts pressed against the plain pajama shirt she wore—that was made decidedly *less* plain because of those breasts—

And fuck, he shouldn't be thinking about *Cora's breasts.*

"You drop that coffee cake, and I'll impale you with this."

He snapped back into his body, into his consciousness. Realized that he had been lost in his perusal of those breasts—and other things—and so he *had* been at risk of dropping the cake. His fork was digging into the pan, tipping it slightly up, and far too near to the edge of the couch for his peace of mind.

One, because the coffee cake from Molly's really was delicious.

Two...because she might really impale him with that fork.

Quickly, he set down his fork, moved the coffee cake to a safe location.

Then he turned his attention to the show. "I'm struggling to understand how this show works."

A flick of her eyes to his. "They buy things at yard sales. They rehab them. Then they sell them, and the team that makes the most money wins."

"I get that part," he said.

Her head swiveled, gaze locking onto his. "Then *why* are you interrupting my binge TV time?"

"Because they're not rehabbing them," he pointed out. "That pair just bought a piece of glass and had the production staff build an entire coffee table around it. That's not rehabbing items from a yard sale. That's...having someone build a brand-new table and then taking credit for it because they set a piece of glass on top."

"Well—"

"And that team," he said, "that locker thing they built is so rickety, I guarantee that it'll fall apart on the drive home if someone is stupid enough to buy it.

"That's not—"

"And—Christ—look at *that!*" He tossed his hands up. "The fucking glass doesn't even fit!"

She smirked. "You're awfully invested in this show for all your moaning and groaning about how bad my choice of TV is."

He shrugged. "But am I wrong?"

"About my choice of TV or the show?"

"Neither."

When she opened her mouth to snark back, he reached around her, stole her Cheetos, managing to get a few out of the bag before she chucked a pillow at his head. Also, she had good aim. Like *really* good aim.

So good that he nearly choked on that first chip, and with all his coughing, he didn't have a chance at blocking her from taking the bag back.

Nor from snatching up the coffee cake.

"You're banned," she muttered.

"Worth it," he wheezed, still trying to not die from the Cheeto dust currently entering his lungs.

"Oh, for God's sake." More muttering, but this time it was paired with her extending her wine glass toward him, putting it up to his lips, and ordering, "Drink."

Then she tilted up the glass, forcing him to drink through his sputtering, and if it didn't soothe the burn and coughing in his throat, he would have thought she was trying to waterboard him with the red wine. But it *did* soothe his choking.

She snatched it away. Put it on the side table—let it be noted that it was well out of his reach. The chips joined it...along with the coffee cake.

He grinned.

She chucked another pillow at him.

"Shut up and watch the damn show."

He didn't realize that she'd nodded off until the soft snore reached his ears.

Then another little puff of sound emerged from her lips.

She still snored the same.

God, she was so fucking cute.

Carefully, he reached across her and snagged the remote, clicking off the TV and cleaning up the mess. And, since she was still snoring, he ate the last bite of coffee cake.

First, it was better fresh.

Second, he'd put one on the counter for the morning.

A total bribe, but he'd taken Teresa's advice and gone to town. There were also two more bottles of wine in her cupboard, flowers in a vase on the island, and six bags of Cheetos in her pantry.

Bribe complete.

He rinsed out her wine glass, put it on the rack, then moved back into the family room. Maybe he should just pull a blanket over her, leave her to her sleep.

But Rafe knew he wouldn't be able to leave her.

He couldn't even leave her house when it would be a hell of a lot smarter to just get a hotel room.

So, he strode across the room, scooped her gently into his arms, and carried her up the stairs.

Down the hall. Into her room. And then he strode over to her bed, tucked her under the covers.

She sighed, nuzzled into her pillow, lips parting.

He wanted to kiss her again.

He wanted to peel back the covers, to slide in behind her. To slip an arm beneath her and to tug her close. To fall asleep with her in his arms. To...wake her up with kisses. To strip off the ratty robe, the adorable pajamas she wore beneath.

To—

Sighing, he smoothed the blanket, tucked it over her a little more securely.

Then he walked from the room.

Even if he needed to force his feet to keep moving the entire time.

Rafe's hands were full. He was trying to carry everything from the table to the sink. His dad liked him when he did that.

Or at least he liked when Rafe did that.

Did things so his dad didn't have to.

But this time he'd tried to do too much, and as he walked to the sink, one of the beer bottles balanced on top of the stack of dishes from the meal he'd made—or the frozen dinner he'd microwaved anyway—toppled from the plate precariously balanced on top.

It fell in slow motion.

Down.

Down.

Down.

And...crash.

Remnants of the beer sloshing out, the bottle shattering, shards going in all directions.

The plates in his arms wobbled, the entire stack threatening to topple, to go down. Scrambling, he managed to keep hold of the dishes, but sauce splattered to the floor...and all over his dad's feet.

"*Fuck,*" he hissed, jumping back. *"Fuck!"* he hissed again, having stepped onto a piece of the glass, and this time he slapped Rafe across the head. Hard enough that Rafe's head snapped back, and he tasted blood. "You're absolutely fucking worthless, you know that?" He lifted his hand again and Rafe closed his eyes, preparing himself for the punch.

But instead, it was a shove.

He stumbled back.

Fell.

Cried out in pain as the dishes clattered in all directions, as the glass bit into his palms, sliced through his jeans.

"Useless," his dad muttered. "Absolutely fucking useless."

"I'm sorry," Rafe said quickly. "I was trying to—"

"Try harder." He kicked a plate, skittering it across the floor, and left, leaving bloody, sauce-covered tracks across the tile. "Clean this shit up."

Rafe looked at his palm, sliced open, the floor, a pile of broken plates, at the sauce and the blood and—

He sat bolt upright, sweat pouring down his face.

"Fuck," he whispered, clamping a hand to his chest. "Fucking hell."

The clock said just after two, but he knew the nightmare would stay with him. It always did. Every *fucking* thing from his childhood always did.

Cursing again, he threw back the covers and stood.

Shower.

Coffee.

Work his ass off to forget.

Make sure the important people in his life knew, *knew* that he wasn't *that*.

Wasn't...worthless.

Eleven

Cora

She had her laptop bag slung over her shoulder, her coffee mug tucked under one arm, a tote with her clothes—it was Thursday Night Friend's Night (which was really just an excuse for prickly pear margaritas, bowls and bowls of chips and queso, and laughter, teasing, and hanging with the people who were most important in her life).

Aside from her brothers and mom, of course.

She also had several files she'd brought home the night before, working in her bedroom and doing her level best to avoid Rafe.

He'd carried her upstairs.

He'd tucked her in.

So tight that she'd felt like a mummy when she'd first woken up the day before...and she'd had to do a fair amount of wriggling and yanking to get free.

Her hair was a mess.

She was late to the office (because her phone had been set to silent—and her alarm turned off—both of which she knew had been done by the man who had tucked her in so securely).

Dale hadn't been happy.

She'd worked late.

So late that Rafe hadn't been up when she'd gotten home, his door firmly closed, light off when she walked quietly down the hall. Which meant that she and her folders and working late had hidden in her room with *her* door firmly closed—though she left *her* lights on.

The better to see her work.

And great, now she sounded like The Big Bad Wolf. *The better to see you, darling.*

Ick.

"You're late."

Dale.

His eyes were filled with irritation, and she found her own eyes drifting to the wall behind his shoulder, to the digital clock that was large enough to be seen from any of the cubes.

"It's six A.M."

"I pay you a salary to be available for me at all times."

Wow.

What?

"I must have missed that clause in my contract," she said, and yeah, it was snarky and a little snappish. To her boss. But honestly, she was done. D.O.N.E. With Dale. With the company.

Dale rocked back on his heels. His brows came up.

His lips parted.

And she didn't give him the chance to say something snarky in return. "I'm going to finish this report," she told him.

Then she moved toward her office.

She glanced back over her shoulder, saw that he'd started to follow her. "In *my* office."

He took another step, as though he were still going trail her.

"Alone," she added firmly.

His brows slammed down, irritation on his face.

But she didn't let that stop her.

Nope. She just moved to the door, closed it with a firm click. Then flicked the lock for good measure.

She took a moment, stifling more teenager-esque sighs, resisting the urge to slam her head on her desk. Mostly because Dale had stopped in front of her office, was staring at her through the blinds adorning her window.

But also, because she needed to have some self-respect, and she wasn't going to let that asshole bother her.

So, she ended her moment.

And got to work.

And after lunchtime rolled around and Dale knocked on her door—or really, thirty minutes before lunch because Dale was Dale—she delivered that report.

And then redid it to his *exacting standards* (which basically meant that she moved two paragraphs around and changed the font).

And *then* the moment she got the fuck out of his space, she went back to her office and spent the rest of the afternoon submitting resumés.

Done.

She was so *fucking* done.

"I think there might be a spot in Heather's department," Kelsey said. "I heard that Abby was looking for someone with marketing experience." She filled up Cora's pitcher with more—what else?—prickly pear margarita. "Do you want me to ask Abby? I'm sure I can get a job description."

"Oh, no," Cora said. "I don't want you to go to any trouble."

"And by *trouble,* you mean sending one email?" Kels's brows lifted. "For my friend."

Cora made a face. "Seriously, *I* left RoboTech in the first place. I don't want to be—"

"Any trouble?" Stef asked.

Innocently.

Except, her lips were twitching.

Cora narrowed her eyes, jabbed a finger in her friend's direction. "I don't want to hear about not making trouble. Not from *you.*"

Heidi grinned. "She's got a point."

More narrowed eyes. "Or *you,*" she muttered. "Ms. I-don't-want-anyone-to-lose-sleep-so-I'll-be-miserably-sick-by-myself."

"That was one time!" Heidi protested. "And during finals week. I didn't—"

"Want to be *any trouble,*" Cora finished for her.

Heidi scowled. "You know, if we hadn't been friends for years, I would think you were really freaking annoying."

"That's the trouble with knowing someone for more than a decade," Cora said innocently, "I know *all* the bad things."

"What bad things?" Brad—Heidi's hubby and the man who was sickeningly in love with her—asked. "My lovely wife has absolutely *no* bad character traits."

Silence.

Then "Boo!"s all around.

Jaime chucked a chip, and with impressive aim, beaned his brother right in the forehead.

"Hey!" Brad snapped. "I'm just trying to compliment my wife here."

"I love my wife, too, but I'd be the first one to admit that she's got a problem with taking in strays."

Animals.

And people.

Which they could all attest to. Kate, her other best friend—

right along with Heidi, Kelsey, and now, Stef—was the type of person who brought people together and kept them together. She was awesome and nice and...well, *awesome*.

"You like my strays," Kate said, looking nonplussed as she sipped her virgin margarita. Jamie stroked a hand over her rounded stomach, and Cora couldn't help but think that his hair had grown out nicely. There had been an incident a few years back with him cutting his man bun because he'd wanted to make a good impression on his wife's family, and the collective of the feminine population had mourned on the altar of deceased sexy man buns (as opposed to gross, greasy ones). She wasn't a woman who liked long hair, but the way he tied it up was totally lumberjack sexy (especially with his bushy beard and bulging biceps and...goddamn, she really needed to get laid).

"You love your wives," Tanner said. "We get it."

Cora and Stef's gazes collided...and their lips twitched. Because Tanner was just as bad.

Which he proved by adding, "Plus, my girl is a certified genius, so she's obviously the best."

"Well, my wife is a mini-genius," Ben said, sliding his arm around the back of Stef's chair and pressing a kiss to the top of her head. "*And* she picks great strays."

Considering that Stef's stray was an adorable golden retriever named Fred, Cora couldn't disagree. Fred was cute. Fred was friendly. As the last single woman standing, Fred had been her date on more than one occasion.

He was attentive and sweet, albeit a bit drooly.

"Did Fred like the new bandana I bought him?" Cora asked, completely off topic and hoping that the interjection would be enough to change the conversation from the menfolk singing the praises of their womenfolk.

As the only single womanfolk, that wasn't great for her ego.

Which was probably why Kate picked up the conversation and ran with it, asking Stef for pictures. Stef produced her phone, and then it was passed around as they all properly admired how handsome Fred was in his big boy bandana.

Talk of the bandana led to talk of Kate and Stef's newest stray, an owner-relinquished chinchilla named Maggie. She was crotchety, didn't like to be held, and had a serious eye infection that vet Jamie was treating. Kate was *treating* the crotchety-ness, and Cora had no doubt that the treatment would be effective.

It wouldn't be long before Maggie would be eating out of Kate's hand.

Probably both literally and figuratively.

Kels nudged Cora's shoulder. "FYI, you pain in the ass—" She grinned. "And I say that with the most love, my darling."

Cora glared, but she knew the picture that she painted—or was attempting to paint, anyway—was ruined when the corners of her lips tipped up.

"FYI," she said again, "I just texted Abby, and she requests that you send your resumé."

"Kelsey," Cora began.

A ping, and then Kels held up her phone, showed Cora the screen. "Like *yesterday*."

"*Kelsey.*"

"Like so much yesterday that she'd love to offer you a job."

She held up the phone again, and Cora saw that Abby had indeed written that. She sighed. "I don't want to manipulate the system—"

"Fuck that."

Cora stopped.

Blinked.

Because that hadn't come out of her mouth (as was most common), nor Kels's or Heidi's or even the slightly quiet, Stef's.

It had come out of Kate's.

Sweet, innocent *Kate's*.

Who glared at everyone's gaping expressions, and even *that* was sweet.

"What?" she asked impatiently. "I curse."

Jaime's face went soft. "Yes, Red, you do."

"Except that you yelled at Tanner last week because he dropped the f-bomb," Heidi pointed out. "You said the baby might hear and have a potty mouth."

"I didn't—"

Cora opened her mouth to agree, but there was movement out of the corner of her eye. The front door opening or maybe it was just a flash of familiarity at the edge of her gaze. Or maybe it was like some part of her was in tune with some part of him.

Him.

Rafe was walking up to the hostess stand, and after a brief conversation, the young blond man there handed him a menu.

She watched his lips move as he read, both hating and loving that she knew he always did that, had always *done* it, all the way back from his elementary school days because he'd struggled with reading and his teacher had helped him and—

His head jerked up.

Their eyes locked.

Her heart began pounding. Her palms went sweaty, and she nearly lost her glass of prickly pear goodness.

"Cor," Kelsey said, and Cora quickly tore her gaze from Rafe's, released a relieved breath when she saw that Kels was looking down at her phone, that the conversation had devolved from pressing her about the job and had moved on to teasing Kate about her cursing habits.

"I've heard that puck is the perfect alternative for the f-bomb," Ben said. "Puck off. Mother pucker. Pucking hell."

"Except hell is a bad word, too," Stef said.

"To whom?" Heidi asked.

"To..." Stef shrugged. "I don't know. To a lot of people."

"I'm telling Abby," Kelsey said, drawing her focus from the curse word alternatives back to her friend's. "I'm telling her that you're sending her your resumé in the morning, so there's no getting out of it now— Wait," she said, suddenly looking up. "Isn't that Rafe?"

Oh, no.

"I don't think so."

Kels leaned to the side. "No, I think it is."

Oh, no.

Kels raised an arm, waved it wildly. "Rafe!"

Oh. *No.*

"Are you ordering takeout?" she called, probably way too loudly considering there were other patrons in the restaurant. "Don't do that! We haven't ordered yet! Come sit with us!"

Cora's eyes slid closed.

Oh. Freaking. No.

Twelve

Rafe

He'd come close without really thinking about it, drawn like a bee to a flower.

Cora's friend waving and calling out just an excuse.

He'd spotted Cora the moment he'd walked into the restaurant.

Slender shoulders revealed in a sleeveless top. Laughter turning her smile warm, drawing him in. He wanted to be the one to make her smile like that. Then she spotted him. And that warmth had disappeared.

Asshole.

Him.

But still his feet had drifted her way.

Then Kelsey had waved in his direction, called him over, and though he should have turned away, forgotten his plan for takeout (and yeah, maybe he'd realized that it was Thursday night and knew she'd be here with her friends, knew that she needed space from him, The Asshole, but he'd come to the restaurant anyway).

They'd avoided each other for a few days.

He was itching to see her.

And when he'd gotten home to that empty house, remembered it was Thursday, he'd come here without really thinking about it.

Or maybe he was thinking *too much* about it.

Because he was at the table, near enough to smell the soft, sweet scent of her, and he was staring.

Not speaking.

Not quipping a funny joke or introducing himself to the people at the table that he didn't know.

Just staring.

At Cora.

Kate—who he'd been introduced to during the margarita night (and who he now knew too much about her attempts at BDSM with her husband, gross)—cleared her throat. "We haven't ordered yet. You want to pull up a chair and sit?"

He was a heartbeat away from saying no, from leaving Cora to her friends and her night.

But then she narrowed her eyes at him and brusquely shook her head.

And...the devil inside him came out.

He turned to the empty table behind him, tugged out a chair, and squeezed it in between her and Kelsey—even though there wasn't room for it, even though Cora definitely didn't want him sliding in next to her. Kels, who he'd met countless times over the years (most of those the elementary ones, since Cora and she had been friends since childhood), grinned.

As he sat, his and Cora's thighs brushed, and though Kels had slid her chair to the side, giving him more space on her side, Rafe didn't shift away from Cora. He stayed *right there*. Thighs pressing together, shoulders in contact, her curls dangerously close to his cheek, his mouth. And her scent surrounding him, dropping him straight into the Cora bubble that promptly made him lose his mind.

Or his words.

Or his mind.

Or his...*something*.

Sanity. Self-preservation. Sense of self.

All the S's.

Because he leaned into Cora's space, that hair of hers smelling like roses and fruit. Maybe it was apples or perhaps pears. All he knew was that it wasn't something tropical. No coconut and bananas and white sand beaches. It was mountains and flannel, the first winter snow, crisp air tightening on cheeks. And...he was a fucking contractor, not a poet (or a bad one since that shit was coming out of his brain). Then a curl brushed across his cheek, and he found himself capturing it between thumb and forefinger, gently tugging as he murmured, "What's wrong, baby?"

She jumped, her shoulder colliding with his, her thigh brushing over the top of his.

Then she leaned back, the curl sliding from his grip, her margarita sloshing over the rim of the glass she held. Her skin glistened with the alcohol, and his mouth watered with the urge to taste the sweet and tart on her flesh, to trace his tongue along that glimmering patch. "*You*, Rafe," she snapped, chocolate eyes sparking fire. "You're annoying and persistent and invading my space." A hiss. "So *that's* what's wrong. And I know that you're smart enough to know that, even though you're playing at being an idiot."

He smirked. "What if I am just an idiot?"

"What if you're both?" she muttered.

"Then I'd suppose I'm exceptionally skilled."

A huff of laughter, and he felt like a fucking superhero when the annoyance faded, and amusement entered her expression.

"Only you would think it's a good thing to be skilled at being an idiot."

"It takes all kinds."

She rolled her eyes. "I could do with a little less of *your* kind."

He chuckled, shifted his thigh against hers, knowing he was playing with fire and unable to stop himself. He was strapped onto the ride, the safety checks complete, and the button had been pushed.

The roller coaster was taking off.

And he was flying...

And he'd deal with the consequences—motion sickness, his friends, her brothers, the complications and anger and fists that would surely be flying—later.

All of that, *later*.

"You know what I think?"

Cora glared. "That I don't care what you think?"

He flashed her a grin, leaned a little closer. "I think you like it when I invade your space."

A sharp inhale.

White teeth pressing into pink lips.

She did. And fuck...he liked it, too.

So much that he was going to get on that roller coaster a second time.

Leaning in further, his lips brushing her ear. "And, full disclosure, I like it, too."

She inhaled again, sharp and short, and then turned her head, eyes hitting his, and her lips coming...so fucking close.

Now he inhaled, smelling the sweet tartness of the margarita, mixing with the apples and fresh snow of her scent. He wanted to taste both on his tongue.

"Rafe," Kelsey said, "I don't know if you've met my husband, Tanner?"

He tore his gaze away from Cora, turned to Kels, saw that

she was looking at him with far too much innocence. Then he glanced from her to the man behind her shoulder, one he'd met a couple of times, but only in passing. Tanner was good-looking, confident, and had been friendly enough. But his focus had been Kelsey because the man was obviously in love and not afraid to show it.

Tanner lifted his chin in greeting.

Before Rafe could return the greeting, his gaze drifted beyond Tanner's shoulder, and he saw the entire table was staring at him. Well, staring at him *and* Cora. And there were more than a few raised brows. And smirks. From the women, that was.

And from the men...

Knowing looks.

Fuck.

If one of Cora's brothers were here, he would be dead. D.E.A.D. *Dead.*

That roller coaster was looking a lot less appealing right about then.

He cleared his throat. "Hi, Tanner," he said, leaning slightly forward in his chair and extending his hand. "Good to see you again."

Kelsey glanced up at her husband, pressed a kiss to the line of his jaw. "I don't know if I told you, Rafe is staying with Cor."

At that, Tanner's brows lifted a little higher.

"In the spare room," Cora burst in, her voice high and squeaking and having those knowing looks spreading from the men to the women.

An awkward pause.

Rafe cleared his throat again. "I have a job in town," he said. "Cora was nice enough to let me crash at her place for a few weeks."

A snort from behind his right shoulder, a feminine thigh shifting against his own.

"What do you do?" one of the other men asked.

"Construction," he said, extending a hand across the table. "I'm Rafe."

"Ben," he said, shaking Rafe's hand firmly. "It's nice to meet you. Stef"—he nodded at the pretty blonde at his side, one Rafe remembered from the night at Cora's house"—mentioned that you were staying at Cora's home."

Ben.

Ben.

Ben *Bradford.*

Holy shit. Rafe hadn't processed who was sitting across the table, and he really should have. Ben Bradford was the newest, hottest tech CEO around. He'd recently taken his company public...and that company had just accepted Rafe's company's bid on a warehouse retrofit.

He mentioned that, and then they began talking shop, which the table allowed for a few minutes before he and Ben were banned from work talk.

"I love you, baby," Stef said. "But it's Thursday Night Friends' Night. Which means there is an expiration label on shop talk."

Ben's face went soft, and he kissed the top of Stef's head, murmured something in her ear that had her cheeks going pink.

"I heard that you got the full Margarita Night Experience," Tanner said.

"Not the *full* experience," Ben chimed in. "There wasn't any alcohol involved."

"It was *enough* of an experience," he said lightly. "Let me tell you that."

Heidi's lips curved. "Did we scar you with our talk of BDSM?"

"Fuck yes, you did," he said, which earned him cackles from all the women except Cora, and sympathetic groans from the men.

Tanner's ears went red. "Please, tell me my wife didn't—"

Rafe put up a hand, palm out. "Let's not go there. Suffice to say, I've bleached any memories of that evening from my brain."

"Fuck, man," he muttered. "These women—"

"Are fabulous and perfect and wonderful," Kelsey interjected with a grin and waggling brows.

Tanner mock glared at her. "And annoying and loud and responsible for sharing far too much and—"

Narrowed eyes directed at Tanner. "And going to get into *so* much trouble—"

Luckily, the server arrived then, two fresh pitchers of margaritas in one hand and a plethora of chip baskets and little cups of queso on a tray that was perched on the shoulder of her free arm. She deposited all of it with an aplomb that told him she had probably taken care of this group before. And he supposed she had, considering that Cora and her friends tried to get together at this restaurant almost every Thursday.

The back-and-forth between Tanner and Kels was halted as glasses were topped off, orders were taken, and then when the server left, her notepad full, Kate jumped right into the conversation, thus preventing the back-and-forth from resuming.

Kate changed the topic of discussion from BDSM and annoying (or perfect, depending on which side of the argument one was part of) women, right to the newest superhero film with an ease that told him both that she'd played this game many a time before and that she was also going to be a really good mom.

As time went on, the conversation was lively (and thank fuck, but there was no more talk of the ladies' sexual habits and/or appetites). They argued about the best villain, made plans to see an action flick. The way the conversation developed and molded and changed was an interesting mix that Rafe had never experienced before—or well, he'd only ever experienced it once. With the Hutchinses. Side conversations and talking across the table interspersed with discussions that included everyone.

Laughter and teasing, warmth and a comfortable familiarity that made him feel about five years old again, escaping the quiet hell that was his house two doors down, and sitting at the table in the Hutchinses' kitchen for the first time.

Cora's mom making up a plate for him without a second glance, not caring that she'd had to pull in a stool from the pantry for him to sit on so he could have a chair.

Then later, after many meals, buying another chair so that he could sit at the table.

He closed his eyes and the conversation continued to roll over him, and he knew the roller coaster had pulled back to the beginning, had come to a halt, unlatched the safety belts. He was gathering his belongings and exiting to the right.

Because...Mrs. Hutchins.

Because Asher and Jeremy and Wyatt, Rome and Eli and Rowan.

How could he move in on their sister when they'd made him one of them? How could he take advantage when they'd done so much?

He was here to look out for Cora. To protect her.

Not too long to see her naked breasts, to taste her...*everywhere*.

A slight clatter in front of him had his eyes flashing open, seeing that the server had placed his beer in front of him.

"Everything okay?" she asked.

He nodded quickly, forced a smile. "Yup. Thanks very much."

But nothing was okay.

His thigh was still pressed to Cora's, their arms occasionally bumping, and even though she had been determinedly ignoring him, he could tell by the stiffness in her frame that she was as aware of him as he was of her.

So, he gave them both a break and scooted his chair from hers, putting some space between them.

Instantly, he felt cold.

But he pushed it down.

Mostly because the conversation was still reminiscent of the Hutchinses, and he wouldn't do anything to jeopardize that.

Even if it felt like he had to shove down part of his heart to get there mentally.

Thankfully, he was helped along by the tears (also an occasional occurrence in the Hutchins household). The waterworks having been caused by Heidi tossing an envelope at Kate. She'd torn it open with furrowed brows, saw what was inside—a pass to a local wild animal park where Kate could hold a sloth (apparently, a lifelong dream for the animal lover that was Kate).

So, before the fajitas had been brought to the table there were tears, Kate alternating between sobbing and squealing and hugging Heidi and Brad (who accepted the gesture but made it clear that it was all Heidi's idea).

Jamie coaxed her back into her seat, wiped the tears away with a tissue he jokingly said that he'd begun keeping in his pocket from the moment he'd learned his wife was pregnant.

Which had earned him a swat from a still-sniffing Kate.

The tears were gone. The glares were back.

And apparently, pregnancy hormones were real.

And also, Cora had good friends.

He liked that for her.

He wished he could like that for *him,* too.

But—the roller coaster took off without him—he knew that wasn't to be.

Thirteen

Cora

She'd had too many margaritas.

Work was going to *suck* tomorrow.

But Kelsey had talked her into sending her resumé over to Abby somewhere between prickly pear margarita three and five and based on the text reply from Abby (*When can you start?*), she didn't think she needed to worry about keeping Dale happy for much longer.

Two weeks.

She would need to keep him happy for two more weeks—or if not happy, then she at least needed to tolerate him for those two weeks.

Because her contract required two weeks' notice.

Because...she was done.

She almost didn't care how much she would be paid or what she would be working on.

She just needed *out.*

Now she was making her careful way to the bathroom. Her car would be spending the night, and she'd ordered a Lyft

—or she'd *attempted* to order a Lyft because Rafe had given her a look, snatched her cell, and ordered her to the ladies' room.

No warmth.

All order. All distance.

Kind of like the space between their bodies. She'd felt him shift away, *seen* the mental shift in the ticking muscle in his jaw, the tension in his muscles. She'd felt the physical one.

A jerk of his chair away.

His thigh shifting from hers. Their arms no longer brushing.

And...she'd felt that distance. And that distance had felt... like a slap.

So, the copious amounts of margaritas and chips and queso, and an entire platter of steak and chicken fajitas. Grilled onions? Yup. Hell, yes. She'd load 'em up, the better to keep annoying, confusing men at bay. Charred peppers? Double hell, yes. If she was feeling a little sick, she might as well add heartburn to the mix.

And heartbreak.

And...her drunk ass was being all dramatic.

That was courtesy of prickly pear margarita five...and also, maybe the gallon of queso she'd downed.

But she was going to focus on the positive.

New job forthcoming.

And it had been the easiest interview process (that being *no* interview process) she'd ever been part of.

Other positives to focus on, however, were a struggle to coax to the forefront of her inebriated mind. Mostly, she could only think of negatives. Like how cold her thigh had felt when he'd pulled away. Like the way he'd almost ignored her after he'd moved his chair. Like the slightly impatient way he'd snagged her phone and told her he'd drive her home.

It hurt.

It shouldn't.

She *should* want that distance. It made things infinitely simpler.

But...part of her liked it when he was close. Okay, a big part of her did. No, if she were being honest, *most* of her did. Most of her wanted to climb him like a cat tower and rub her face against his. Cover him with her scent, soak in his.

And *that* was the margaritas talking.

Bathroom.

She'd come into the bathroom to *use* the bathroom, and that meant she needed to stop staring at herself in the mirror and actually do her business.

Not think about how much she'd liked the kiss and the gruff way he'd wanted to protect her. How he'd chucked her shoes and made her hot cocoa because he knew it would help her sleep. How he'd gotten mad about the long hours and then kissed her in a way that had her not feeling like a boring little sister.

But like a woman.

Heart-pounding, lungs screaming, a hear-her-roar *woman.*

And a melting puddle of desire.

That too.

"Bathroom," she told her reflection. "Get on it."

She concentrated—because margaritas—on her business then washed her hands and pushed out into the hall, nearly plowing into Rafe.

"Easy," he said, his hands coming to her hips as he steadied her.

She stiffened.

Because she knew what was going to happen next.

And yup—the moment he processed that he was touching her—he jumped back, clenching his hands into fists at his sides.

She hitched her purse up higher on her shoulder, feeling more and more sober by the second. She wanted to order another pitcher of margaritas, to allow the pleasant fog of alcohol to suck her under again.

Anything was better than the slice of pain those clenched fists wrought.

Anything was better than feeling *this.*

God.

Pathetic.

She needed to grab on to her inner Cora. The tough, badass who didn't put up with any shit, and who knew her own head and heart. Lifting her chin, she pushed past him. "I need to get my bag out of my car before we go."

Then she walked down the hall, pushed out the back door, and strode across the back patio.

It was one of her favorite places with twinkly lights and a dance floor and had been the perfect space for Kate and Jaime's wedding.

Smiling, as she thought about that night and how happy her friends had been, how much fun they'd all had (despite an unfortunate cake disaster wrought by Heidi and Kate's trouble-making rooster, nicknamed The Fuzz), she moved quickly across the quiet space.

It was late and the tables had been bussed, the chairs stacked along the edge of the dance floor.

She pushed through the little gate on the far side of the space and bleeped the locks on her car, Rafe a thundercloud of a presence behind her left shoulder.

She tugged open the driver's door. "I can just—"

"You're *not* driving."

A breath through her nose. "I didn't say that I was going to drive." She snagged her bag from the passenger's seat, straightened, slinging it over her shoulder. "I was going to offer to get a Lyft."

"To the same house?" He grabbed the bag from her, slung it over *his* shoulder.

And that was it.

He spun, walked toward his truck, crammed into a spot in the far end of the lot, opened the passenger's side door.

Waited.

Cora stood there, debating walking the miles between there and home versus getting in that damn truck...and knowing there was no point in debating because he would get her ass in that truck.

Plus, it was cold, and she was tired, and she didn't *want* to walk home.

Which was why she walked over to the truck.

Okay, maybe she stomped, but just a little bit.

One foot on the running board, another inside the cab. She reached for the handle, started to draw herself up and in and—

Then her lungs froze.

Because he was touching her again.

Lifting her into the seat. Then jerking back his hands like he'd just completed the most disgusting action ever, like he needed to go dunk himself into a bucket of bleach.

Nice.

The door closed.

And so did her eyes.

At least if her lids were shut, she could pretend her world hadn't gotten so twisted and tangled, could pretend there wasn't hurt woven into every breath of her interactions with Rafe. She didn't even *like* him. He was an adoptive brother and nothing more, so it shouldn't hurt that he wasn't touching her like a woman he wanted, as he had in her kitchen.

Except...it did.

It hurt down to the marrow of her bones, felt like a stake in the heart, acid in her stomach...or well, an acid that didn't belong there. One that burned and had the contents churning and made her hate herself.

Because fuck him.

She didn't allow any man to drudge up those feelings in her.

Not now, not ever.

Not. *Ever.*

The last she remembered was feeling like shit.

Then she woke up, floating through the air, bouncing against something uncomfortably hard.

Spice in her nose. Strong arms surrounding her.

And for all her pretending to hate the feelings Rafe brought out, to despise the annoying, over-the-top way he was trying to shove them into the brother and sister roles…she liked it.

Nothing was better than when he was holding her.

Nothing.

Which made her a total pathetic weakling, she knew.

Something else that added to that weakling status?

The fact that she closed her eyes and continued to pretend to be asleep. Through the walk up to the house, through his bumbling with the lock and up the stairs. Her eyes stayed closed as he carried her down the hall and tucked her into bed.

Gentle fingers removed her shoes, tugged the covers up, and smoothed them lightly over her shoulders.

The light clicked off.

The door closed softly.

His footsteps padded away.

But her heart, as stupid as it was, her heart went right with him.

They met in the kitchen and squared off like enemies on opposite sides of the battlefield.

She threw up the white flag.

Mostly because she hadn't been able to sleep after her catnap in the car, and during her sleepless hours, she'd decided (and maybe it had been delirium that fueled this decision) to take a page out of Rafe's book.

She'd pretend.

She'd pretend he was just another one of the big lugs that were her brothers, and then everything would be fine.

So, yeah, she was totally ostriching.

But sometimes a girl had to be an ostrich.

"Coffee?" she asked, even though she was already making him a to-go mug.

Silence, as though weighing if this were a trap.

Then, footsteps growing closer, "Yeah. Thanks, Cor."

She shrugged, snapped the lid on, and set it to the side, filling her own mug and adding copious amounts of sugar and creamer because...she needed the sugar and creamer to deal with this *and* the forthcoming interaction with Dale.

Abby had emailed her early that morning with a formal offer.

Cora had signed it, sent it off, and in two weeks' time, she would be a RoboTech employee again. (Also, this just in, fuck startups run by middle-aged, mediocre men, she'd take Heather O'Keith as a CEO any day of the week).

"This one for me?"

Cora blinked, glanced from her mug to the one Rafe was reaching for and nodded.

"You need to run off to work or you got time for breakfast?" he asked, his eyes searching hers, probably looking for something that wasn't there. Okay, hopefully, it wasn't there. It being the longing, the revisiting the kiss and the shoe toss in her mind at increasingly inconvenient times.

Like right then.

She shoved it down. "I need to go get my car."

He rested a hip against the counter, arms lazily crossed, one hand gripping the mug where it rested against the shelf of biceps.

Convenient, that.

And, yes, she was also aware that thinking about Rafe's biceps went against her thinking of him as an annoying lump of older brotherness.

But...best intentions.

But...baby steps.

But—

"No, you don't."

She blinked, her hand gripping her own mug. "Um, did you forget that you drove me home last night?"

"Nope." He took a long drink from his cup, and no, she definitely didn't watch the strong lines of his throat work as he swallowed, didn't note his biceps flexing and shifting as he lifted it.

"So, unless my car is like an errant puppy finding her way home..."

He lowered the mug, reached one hand into his back pocket, and tossed her...

Her keys.

"I went and got it last night."

Her brows were drawn so tightly together that she could actually feel the furrows imprinting themselves on her forehead, but he enlightened her before she could ask.

"Caught a Lyft to the restaurant, drove it here."

How had she not heard the garage door open or the car pull up?

She hadn't slept...or at least she hadn't thought so. Maybe the man had ninja skills. Or maybe she had just been so lost in the tornado of her brain that she hadn't heard him.

It didn't matter.

What did was that her car was here, she had a new job on the docket, and...in front of her was the perfect opportunity to reinforce to her stupid, stupid brain that Rafe was nothing more than a brother.

So, she nodded. "Thanks."

And then she accepted his offer for breakfast, sat at the island while he made her favorite cinnamon sugar toast, and when he plunked the plate down next to her before plunking his butt up onto the counter by her elbow while shoveling plain buttered toast into his mouth telling her about his job and asking her cautious questions about hers (then more excited ones when she mentioned the job Kels had basically maneuvered for her), she could almost pretend that he *was* just Rafe.

Just another brother.

If only her heart didn't skip a beat when he slid down, his hip brushing her shoulder.

FOURTEEN

RAFE

Teresa's gaze scanned the plans, and he waited to see what she would come up with.

They'd spent the day with the construction team from Ben's company, going over supplies and timelines, and then they'd popped over to the warehouse.

For his new pet project.

This would become something that was his, something he'd get to make all the decisions on from start to finish.

Well, all the decisions that weren't changed or nixed by Teresa.

Right.

Anyway.

He did the big jobs with businesses so he could do the passion projects that fed his soul. And since Teresa always seemed to get exactly what fed his soul—at least in a business capacity—he was fine with her nixing the ideas that wouldn't fit in with his plans for the project.

"You know," she said, tracing her finger over the layout of

what he'd envisioned would be the gym area, "between this and our other current projects, plus the bids that have been accepted, you're looking at more than two years of work here in the Bay Area."

That was his goal.

Or, well, he wanted to shift things from the Central Valley and SoCal to the Bay Area.

One, because he was tired of traveling.

Two, because his foreman for the SoCal jobs, Cabe, hadn't been nearly as effective at finding work as Teresa and Steve (his lead in the Central Valley). That had been before Rafe had let him go, having caught him giving kickbacks to shoddy subcontractors. He'd managed to relocate most of the crew to Steve and Teresa's teams as he finished off the contracted jobs, but that meant he'd spent a lot of time in the Valley lately.

And he wasn't a fan of the traffic and smog and *traffic* of Southern California.

Not that there wasn't traffic in the Bay Area.

It was just...it felt more like home.

And it was closer to the Hutchinses. Or at least, closer to Cora's mom's new house at the foothills of the Sierras, and since whatever Hutchins were in town tended to get together on the regular (and since he was an honorary Hutchins himself), he wanted to be close to the action.

Or Cora.

He clenched his jaw.

Cora was a Hutchins. *That* was why he wanted to be close. Not the only reason, but definitely near the top of the list.

"That's a good start," he said, ignoring that thought. "Between this and the jobs Steve pulled, the company is going to have its best year ever."

"Right."

He waited for her to say more or to comment on the *best year* thing.

But the only thing she did was look at him expectantly.

"What?" he finally asked.

"You realize that this means you should probably start looking for your own place, right?" One side of her mouth kicked up. "I know you said you bribed your way back into her good graces with wine and baked goods, thank me very much"—she blew on her knuckles, buffed them on her shoulder—"but I don't think she'd be down with letting you live in her guest room for two-plus years."

"I'm going down to finish up the job in a couple of weeks," he pointed out.

Teresa nodded. "Well, all I'm saying is that when you come up a few weeks after that, you should probably have a plan to live somewhere else." She made an X on the plans, sketched out a new layout of a few offices. "And, no, that's not me offering up *my* spare room."

"I'm only staying there because her brothers..."

The look she shot him had the rest of his words drying up in his throat.

"Only because of her brothers?"

"Well"—he reached over her, used his pencil to expand on what she was doing with the offices—"because of her, too," he said and added before the triumphant look Teresa could send his way could manifest into something that took over the conversation, or more than it already was, anyway—"You should have heard about the last guy she dated. He pounded on her door at midnight, demanding another chance. What if he'd gotten inside? What if—"

"She'd just call the police and take care of her own shit, like she is very capable of doing?"

He stopped, closed his mouth so fast that his teeth clicked together.

"I know you and her brothers have this weird sense of protectiveness that should have gone away like, fifteen years ago, but I've met Cora. Many times over the last few years. She's fully capable of running her own life without you guys meddling in it."

"I know that, but—"

"Do you?'

He frowned.

"Do you actually know that?" she asked. "Because it doesn't appear that way to me and coming as a woman who is the baby of the family with an extremely overprotective brother and sister herself, all I know is that sooner or later Cora is going to lose patience with all this."

"She already has." More times than he could probably think of.

Usually, this resulted in her calling in Mama Hutchins, who did some threatening—mainly involving food, because the Hutchins boys loved their food. Hell, one year, she and Cora went to Tahoe for Thanksgiving without telling anyone and left them to try to rustle up their own meal for the holiday.

That was the year that Rafe had learned how hard it was to cook a turkey.

They'd eaten Chinese food.

Because it was the only restaurant that was open and had shared a store-bought pumpkin pie that Asher had managed to wrestle away from another desperate man.

"Well, if she has, and you guys haven't listened, then watch out."

They finished sketching, so he rolled up the plans, tapped the end on his thigh to even it out. "What do you mean?"

"I *mean*, at some point, all this meddling is going to cause Cora to lose it, and then you guys are at risk of losing *her*. Forever."

A sick feeling exploded in his gut, spiraling up and out until the back of his throat burned.

"That scares you."

Of course, it did. "She's like a sister—"

Teresa snorted.

"—to me."

She huffed out a breath, patted him on the shoulder. "Right," she said. "So, if that's truly the case, then why do you look like you're going to puke right now?"

He inhaled sharply, but she didn't give him a chance to answer, just shook her head, called out a goodbye, and then she was gone.

And all he could think was, if she could see what he was trying to hide, even from himself, then what would Cora's brothers see?

Useless?

Worthless?

And even if not that, then how painfully would they kill him for daring to touch her?

He stayed in the warehouse long after Teresa left, walking the space, using the excuse of needing to feel the vibe with the changes in the layout they were making, but truthfully, he wasn't noticing the vibe or anything else.

It was all white walls and emptiness.

And Cora.

And Asher and Jeremy and Rome and Rowan and Wyatt and Eli.

Would he lose one or the other?

Or would he lose them all?

But if he continued pretending he didn't have feelings for Cora, what *else* would he lose?

And maybe, maybe if he really worked at it, proved his worth, did all the right things, he could make both work?

Sighing, he eventually sank down onto the floor and rested

his head against a wall that was soon to be taken out, looking at the space and feeling absolutely disgusted with himself.

For myriad reasons.

But really, it all came down to one thing.

Was he going to be able to shove down the feelings for Cora, to only see her as a sister? Or was he going to risk it all and tell her how he felt?

He knew it would be good.

That kiss had been...

And he wasn't risk averse. Rafe had done more than a few stupid things, starting with jumping off really big rocks into a questionably deep lake as a child and ending with moving his business up into a competitive market because he missed his real family.

(That being the Hutchinses).

It was just...he had a family that was bad, and he was part of one that was fantastic. So, knowing how bad *bad* could be, and how good *good* could be, how could he even think of risking being part of the Hutchins family on something that was probably a fad, a weird out-of-the-blue urge that would go away as quickly as it came on?

He couldn't.

He just...couldn't.

Further that, he was going to take Teresa's advice and make sure the collective brothers—himself included—stepped back the overbearingness and stopped interjecting themselves into Cora's life. They needed to let her live it.

Because he couldn't lose her either, even if it meant keeping her in a way that was a sad facsimile of what he really wanted.

Of course, what he *didn't* know as he sat there, making those plans, was that the moment he got back to her place, all of that would go to absolute shit.

Fifteen

Cora

Breakfast that morning had told her one thing.

She needed to keep living her life.

Lunch in her office with Dale alternating between firing her and begging her to stay had prompted her to lose herself in her phone.

In the *apps* on her phone.

And she wasn't in Safari playing Wordle (which, btw, she'd kicked ass by getting it on the second guess that morning, so bam!).

She was dusting off her dating apps.

Refreshing her profile, swiping, and...matching.

Messaging. With a guy who was cute, lived in the area, and had adorably asked if it was too soon to take her out for a drink that evening.

Not in a pushy way either.

But...endearing and making her smile and considering Dale's alternating fury and pressure and mood swings that had her seeing stars, *and* Rafe's deliberately brotherly distance, endearing and eager was much appreciated.

So was the drink.

If it went well, it could turn into something more.

If it went poorly, she could peace out.

If she wanted to bust out the handcuffs and rock Donovan's (cute name, right?) world, then she could do just that.

She was a grown woman—or maybe that was *groan* woman because the moment she had opened her garage door and was making her way to her car, Rafe pulled up to the curb. She was meeting Donovan at a local bar because she was a grown (not groan) woman and didn't want a strange man showing up at her house or knowing where she lived.

His truck turned off, and she heard the door open and close.

And yeah, she hurried for her car, to open *her* door, to get inside before he saw what she was wearing.

Which was short and tight and paired with high, high heels and red lips and smoky, shimmering eyes.

She looked hot.

She *looked* ready to fuck.

And she just might. If Donovan were cute enough and nice enough and she felt like it.

But she really didn't want to deal with Rafe.

This dress, these heels would ensure that she would be dealing with him.

His footsteps reached the garage just as she tugged the handle and started opening the door.

"What. The. Fuck?"

She glanced over her shoulder, ignored the heat that began bubbling through her middle, dripping down to gather between her thighs when she saw his gaze on her ass, as it traced slowly up her legs. And she knew a lot of them were on display with the short hem, just like there was a lot of the *rest* of her on display in her backless dress.

His stare was almost a physical caress. She felt it hit the bare skin between her shoulder blades, caress over her hair (curls on display and looking fucking good, thank her very much).

Then the air in her lungs went solid.

Because his eyes had hit hers.

Fire.

Need.

He stepped closer. No. He stepped *close,* pinning her between the car and his chest, hot breath on her nape, scorching words in her ear. She shivered, and he leaned more heavily against her. The cool metal of her car. The heat of his chest.

Thunk.

She turned her head, saw one broad hand plunking onto the car's frame.

Thunk.

The other boxing her in on the other side.

Thunk.

His body shifted, his knee closing the door, his body shifting even closer.

"Where are you going?"

Her body was practically vibrating with awareness, but she managed to get an answer out. "I have a date."

Still.

He was so fucking still.

Then he was leaning a little closer, his head dropping to her throat as he inhaled deeply. Her gaze was still facing forward, and she watched his hands tighten, the knuckles standing out in sharp relief. Why? Why was that so fucking sexy, that show of obvious strength?

She shivered again, and with him so close, the movement brought her ass in contact...

With him.

With *all* of him.

Sweet Jesus, she'd had some cock in her life, *good* cock. But

Rafe was packing, and the way that he rolled his hips, just a slight press, a rhythmic motion, she knew he knew how to use it.

Instinct drove her to arch back, not slightly this time, but to get the full feel of him.

And for one glorious second, he moved into her, made her wonder if angels were singing, or if it were actually possible to come from a man just thrusting into her ass and not touching any of the pertinent parts.

With Rafe and his clenching hands and big cock nestled right between her cheeks, she thought it might just be possible.

Another thrust.

Not exactly gentle, but she liked the edge of rough, the thought that he might be losing just the slightest bit of control.

It was hot.

So fucking hot that with the next thrust, her arms wrapped around his, palms gripping his wrists, ass up, spine arched, a moan tumbling from her lips.

So good. That felt so fucking good that she didn't notice the change in him, not right away.

Not until his hips shifted away.

Not until he'd tugged his arms free of her grip.

Not until his mouth had dropped to her ear again.

"Have a good time on your date," he whispered.

Cora blinked, desire having made everything go slightly fuzzy, trying to process those words, the meaning, and when she did, hurt slicing down her spine, tangling in her middle with shame and self-chastisement, she pulled away, smacking her front against the car.

She stumbled, caught herself just in time to see him climbing the two stairs that led into the house, moving like he wasn't the least bit affected.

And, right then, she hated him.

Just a little bit.

Just—

He pushed open the door, glanced over his shoulder. "And don't forget a jacket," he said, tone so neutral it had her teeth clenching together.

Then opening, a retort on the tip of her tongue—

"It's cold out tonight."

The door closed.

Her retort stayed on her tongue.

And, right then, she hated him, more than just a little bit.

She was turning into an alcoholic.

And it was all Rafe's fault.

Donovan was a nice guy. He was as cute as his picture, polite, and not pushy. And he was into her. Into her in a way that didn't have him clenching his fists and running away from her.

So...she'd accepted his offer to drive her home when one drink had turned into three, along with appetizers and desserts while sitting at Bobby's.

He turned off the engine, spun to face her. "I'll walk you up."

"You don't have—"

"I know I don't." He grinned at her. "But if I don't, I won't get a chance at a goodnight kiss without the console jamming into my side."

That made her giggle. Not solely because of the drinks—though she could freely admit that the drinks encouraged it—but because Donovan had been making her laugh all night. He was a manager at a popular club in town, and he had *all* the stories about people behaving badly (which, not ironically, was her favorite subReddit ever).

He grinned, popped open his door, and strode around the hood, getting to her side just as she started to push out, catching her hand and drawing her up. He closed the door, looped his arm around her side, and said, "Nice house."

"Thanks."

"I'm more of an apartment guy," he said as they wove through her planters. "Mostly because I have a black thumb."

She smiled up at him. "This"—she waved a hand at the planters, perfectly lit, exactly as Kate had planned—"is courtesy of my brothers and my friends."

"Nice friends."

"Yeah," she said softly as they reached the porch.

"Nice night," he said, just as softly.

Her lips curved. "That's a lot of *nices*."

"Truth?"

She nodded.

"You're so beautiful that it's hard to think sometimes, and that goes double for trying to think up adjectives."

Cora inhaled, her eyes prickling because that was...*nice*.

"Cora?"

"Yeah?"

"Okay if I kiss you goodnight?"

She nodded.

His lips curved, and then he lowered his head, brushing his mouth over hers once. Twice.

Oh, that was...nice.

But just *nice*, just nice and a little boring, and nothing at all like she felt when Rafe had kissed her—

Don't think about Rafe.

Right. No Rafe.

Just her and Donovan and his mouth and his tongue that was a little *too* much tongue. But the way he held her was *nice*, and it didn't leave her any doubt that he liked her, liked what they were doing and was excited by it.

The problem was...her response was only slightly better than lackluster.

"Donovan." She tore her mouth from his. "This isn't—"

The door opened.

They both jumped, and she glanced to her right to see—sigh—*Rafe* silhouetted in the light from the hall, his arms crossed over his chest, his expression thunderous.

Donovan froze, his hands still gripping her ass, his mouth still close enough that she could feel his breath puffing on her lips.

"Really?" Rafe asked, eyes on hers.

"This is none of your business."

Donovan's hands started to drop, brows shooting up. "Is this one of your brothers?"

Considering she was black and Rafe was white—very white—she thought this was a pretty dumb question, but she didn't say anything because it was late and she was tired, and hell, he might as well have been her adoptive brother, so what the hell did she know?

"No," she said. "Rafe isn't my brother."

Donovan's brows went higher. "Your roommate?"

She pressed her lips together. "Not exactly."

"So...is he your man?" he asked.

"It's not like that," she began. "He's—"

Donovan grinned, shrugged, and said, "Hey, no judgment here. You're a beautiful woman with needs. If he's game for an open relationship, who am I to complain?" His hands tightened, drawing her closer, his pelvis brushing hers.

And for the record, what he was packing didn't compare to Rafe.

"That's not what—"

"I'm just saying"—his hands dipped down again, drew her even more tightly against him—"I'm happy to join in whatever activities are on the table."

She turned her head away, and unfortunately, that meant she met Rafe's stare.

His brows lifted. "*This* is what you want?"

Like she was sexually attracted to dog shit.

And look, she was all for the *you-do-you* mentality, especially when it came to what happened between the sheets.

But she wasn't much for sharing, and yeah, maybe she'd read more than her fair share of MM or MMF books, and she couldn't say she hadn't had the odd fantasy here or there about being with two guys at the same time. But that was just it. Those thoughts were a fantasy, and despite Donovan's offer, she couldn't imagine trying to tackle two men at once.

"Hey, man," Donovan said, his fingers kneading her ass in a way she probably would have liked if not for the offer in the air, if not for Rafe and the way he was staring at her (the dog shit sexual attraction). But Rafe was there, so when Donovan went on, she was ready for the floor to open up and swallow her whole. "I'm just here for the lady, but I'm also good to just watch or be watched or—"

"Shut up."

Donovan shut up.

"Cor?" Rafe asked.

Her gaze shot up to the man standing in the doorway, now staring at her expectantly.

Wanting her to answer the question.

Waiting for her to give that answer.

She *should* want Donovan. Okay, maybe not *should* want him. She *wanted* to want him because that meant she wouldn't want Rafe. And maybe it would also rub in his face that she was a sexy and desirable woman and—

Her sigh was silent.

Attraction and chemistry couldn't be faked, and as *nice* as Donovan was, the draw just couldn't compare...

"*Cor?*"

To Rafe.

His green eyes glimmered.

"Do you want him?" he asked bluntly.

And her answer was just as blunt.

"No," she whispered.

Donovan's arms jerked.

She winced, not because it hurt, but because she wasn't the kind of woman who brought one man home, only to drop him for another. "I'm sorry," she said softly.

To his credit, Donovan didn't get mad. "Nice plants. Nice house. Nice woman." He cupped her cheek. "No guilt." A kiss to her cheek, whispered words in her ear. "But I don't think you're one for an open relationship." He straightened slightly, tilted his head in Rafe's direction. "And I don't think he is either."

Her gaze went to Rafe again, to the rage emanating off him.

"Bye, Cora." There was an edge of disappointment in Donovan's voice, but that was as far as it went before he released her, nodded in Rafe's direction, and left, his car zipping off down the road mere moments later.

And...silence.

Tension. Anger.

Waves and waves of it pulsing off Rafe, coursing over her.

And all the while, he just stared at her, those eyes as effective as stakes pinning her in place. Which was why she didn't move into the house, didn't do anything but watch Rafe's hands open and close, open and close.

But eventually, the silence got to be too much.

"I had to leave my car again," she whispered.

"I know," he said, eyes flicking behind her then coming back to hers.

"I'm not drunk." Still whispering. "I'm just...not sober."

Her gaze dropped to his hands again, saw that they'd clenched into fists again. Tight skin, white knuckles. Strong capable hands that had helped her with her house, held her tight, but were also gentle to tuck her into bed, to make her cinnamon toast.

Silence had her gaze drifting up to his.

"I'm not drunk," she said again.

"I know," he said the moment their eyes connected.

"I—"

The rest of whatever she'd been about to say was caught up in a gasp because suddenly Rafe was there, and by *there,* she meant he was in her space, sweeping her up into his arms, and...and...

Those hands went to work, holding her tight.

Pleasure slid through her.

No.

It consumed her, set her on fire, burned through her nerves, set her heart skittering. Had *her* hands going to work, gripping his shoulders, sliding up so that one covered his nape and the other shoved itself into his hair.

"Cora," he groaned.

"Rafe." A whisper.

A plea.

And finally, finally he obliged.

His mouth covered hers, tongue thrusting deep.

One of his hands went to her ass, slid down her thigh, coaxing it around his hip, and she quickly wrapped both legs around him, lungs screaming, head spinning, tongue doing its level best to keep up with his.

Then they were moving.

Into the house, up the stairs, cool air on her legs, a hot palm dipping under the hem of her dress and cupping her bare ass cheek.

Warm rough hands.

Fingers dipping just slightly into her crack.

And seriously, thongs for the win.

Down the hall.

Into her room.

Onto...she squealed when her ass collided with cold granite.

Into the bathroom apparently.

His emerald eyes blazed with need, his lips were swollen, his chest rose and fell like he'd run a marathon. But all he did was reach for her toothbrush, slap some toothpaste on it, and order, "Wash him off."

She shivered.

And not from the cold tile.

But she didn't grab the toothbrush.

A spark of fury, fueling the desire coursing through her. It dripped down her thighs, had her pussy absolutely aching.

She grabbed the toothbrush. She scrubbed her teeth. She spat and rinsed and—

Another squeal as she was in his arms again. But it was only a millisecond long because then his mouth was on hers again, and she wasn't thinking about Donovan or how much she liked bossy Rafe in the bedroom.

She was flying through the air, landing with a slight *oof* on the mattress—

And Rafe was between her thighs.

A jerk brought her ass to the edge of the bed.

A rough movement to spread her wide.

He gripped her panties, yanked, and...they were gone. The silk fluttering to the floor somewhere behind him. She hadn't even known it was possible to do that. Hell, she didn't think it *was* possible to actually tear someone's panties off.

But Rafe had and...

Wet.

She'd been wet before, dripping down her legs. Now...now she was practically melting for him.

And he was kneeling before her, lips parting, eyes glued to her bared pussy.

Sixteen

Rafe

He was going to hell, and he couldn't summon a fuck to give about it.

Glistening folds, shorn curls, lush legs spread wide.

And Cora in that dress that revealed more than it covered, the hem dancing around her ass, the top so low cut that her tits were nearly bursting free as she lifted herself up onto her elbows and stared down at him.

With mischief in chocolate eyes.

"You just going to look at it?" she murmured.

He was tempted to.

"It *is* the prettiest pussy I've ever seen," he said, stroking a finger through her folds.

So. Fucking. Wet.

Like a knife through butter, and he knew that he'd slid right into the hot, tight clasp of her. No resistance. Just liquid silk.

Cora's head tipped back, her throat on display and calling for his mouth.

But the part in front of him was calling louder.

He drew his finger back down, tracing patterns through her labia, slowly making his way back up to her clit, pressing lightly.

A gasp. A curse. Her thighs shaking. Her hips thrusting up.

His head dipped. He inhaled.

And...he lost control.

Hands beneath her ass and drawing her close, yanking her against his mouth, thrusting his tongue deep inside, his thumb sliding up, circling her clit, pressing firmly.

And...Cora lost control.

She bucked against him, thighs clenching around his head so tightly he almost couldn't breathe, the mattress bouncing when her elbows gave way and she caught his hair, holding him to her. Fine by him. He was prepared to drown in her.

But first, he needed to get her off, to see her come apart for him.

He needed to know everything about her.

What touches sent her soaring. What words pushed her over the edge. Did she like his tongue—

Oh yeah. She definitely liked his tongue there.

Firm kisses and gentle circles.

But suction. Suction was where it was at for her.

"Shit. Rafe. Oh fuck!" Her hips ground against his mouth, her hands gripped tighter. Hell, that stung. He would be surprised if he had any hair left when he was done, and truthfully, he wouldn't give one fuck if he ended up with two bald patches by the time he made her come.

Not that he gave a fuck.

Because he'd be making her come.

Because...

Thoughts left him as he became a machine focused on making sure she reached the precipice, that she toppled over the edge. He drank her up, sucked her harder, deeper, pressed a finger home at the same time as he hauled her closer to him.

Her breath caught.

One breast popped free from her dress.

The sight of her nipple, beaded and calling for his mouth had him doubling down, moving faster, circling and licking, kissing and sucking and—

She came apart on his mouth, a gush of liquid on his tongue.

Tart berries, sweet Cora.

Her hair was splayed around her shoulders, her eyes were half-mast. Her other breast was threatening to escape, and fuck yeah, when she took a deep breath, his wish came true, and it popped free. Dusky nipples. Jiggling breasts. Glistening skin.

The *fucking* best.

"Rafe," she whispered, lifting her head enough that those heavy, half-mast eyes collided with his. "Please."

He moved, lifting her up as he shifted onto the bed, her head hitting the pillow, lips parting on a gasp. He wanted to taste that gasp, but his fingers were already working on more important things, tugging down the rest of her dress, leaving her bare to his gaze, and fuck, she was gorgeous. Breasts and hips and skin that demanded to be kissed.

"Wait," she said as he started to climb over her, intending to start with her mouth and then kiss her all the way down.

"No?" he asked, knowing he'd stop, but really not wanting to.

His cock hurt it was so hard. His hands shook and his mouth watered and sweat had broken out on his spine. He needed her, and he needed her *now,* and he needed to have her before the rest of the world intruded.

Before he thought about that fucker who'd escorted her up onto the porch, about their family, and her brothers and—

"Yes," she said, "I just—"

Her hands went to the hem of his shirt, began tugging it up, and he understood.

Rearing back, he yanked it over his head, shifted so he could shove off his pants, his underwear.

Her gasp, her eyes widening in approval, lips parting, and what he wouldn't give to have them parting because she was taking his cock between them.

The thought had barely formed before she was up on her knees, her hands coming to his chest.

A shove had him falling back, narrowly missing the foot-board, but then she was on him, straddling his middle, hands on his shoulders as she bent and kissed him deeply. Her tongue was in his mouth, tangling with his. Her pussy was splayed across his stomach, the damp heat of her arousal soaking into his skin. Hands in his hair, breasts on his chest, nipples hard and dragging across his skin.

And that was enough for his control to splinter.

He flipped them, coming on top of her, and finally, *finally* got his mouth on her breasts, and hell yeah, he discovered that she loved suction there, too, drawing on her nipple, rolling the other between thumb and forefinger. Then palming her breast, caressing and squeezing lightly, before dragging his palm down her side, dipping his fingers between her legs again.

A hiss as he brushed his thumb over her clit.

Her thighs clenching around his arm, but he didn't stop.

Just continued stroking as he kissed his way to her other breast, lavished it with attention until her hips started working against his hand, until liquid silk began to gather on his palm, his fingers. Her hands came to his head, tugged him off her breasts, drawing him up, slanting her mouth across his and kissing him so deeply that he felt as though his heart was going to pound out of his chest.

"Now," she broke away, gasping. "Now, Rafe."

He didn't think.

Didn't *think*.

Just spread her thighs and thrust deeply.

Oh fucking hell. Tight and wet, her pussy clasping around his dick. She arched against him, wound her legs around his hips as he moved once, twice, felt his orgasm coil at the base of his spine. That was the moment he knew he'd better get her there and fast, because if she wasn't *there* with him, then she'd be shit out of luck.

So, he needed to figure out what she liked.

And he needed to do it quickly.

Hitching her leg up, he thrust several times, clenching his teeth to hold back his desire as he found out what she liked, what angle had her gasping, what pressure had her neck curving as she *thunked* her head back into her pillow.

"Oh God, baby," she moaned. "Just like that. Like *that.*"

Thank fuck.

He kept like *that*, thrusting deep and hard and clenching his teeth, and feeling sweat drip down his spine and her lips parted, his name toppling off her tongue.

"Come, baby," he ordered. "Come for me."

Come before he did.

A hard thrust, deeper than before.

Her pussy convulsed, a moan bubbled up in the back of her throat, and...*there*. Thank fuck, she came, gripping him so tightly that his orgasm barreled forward, that he exploded, pounding into her, barely able to make sure he wasn't hurting her, that the thrusting was extending her pleasure and not hindering it.

Then he wasn't thinking of anything else.

Then he was *feeling*.

Then he was lost in the sensation of Cora.

How good it felt to have her wrapped around him, how perfect this moment was, how perfect *she* was.

And then...he lost sense of himself, of the world, of time and place.

Seventeen

Cora

Her heart pounded against her ribs.

Sweat coated her skin.

And every muscle was lax and loose and like putty.

The best sex of her life, and it hadn't even involved handcuffs.

A giggle bubbled up in her chest and burst through her lips. The man was still on top of her, still inside her, a hot, hard brand (and hey, giggling with him deep inside her felt great, no lie).

He stiffened.

And reality intruded.

She went stiff, the pleasure that had been inundating her faded away. Because...reality. Certainly, it was hitting Rafe, too, and any moment he was going to be pushing up and off her, pulling out and leaving her cold and empty and—

He shifted, pulled out, slid off her.

Cora's heart squeezed, and she mentally braced as he pushed to his feet.

Waited for him to go.

But then his fingers were around her wrist, and he was tugging her to the edge of the bed, scooping her up into his arms, carrying her to her bathroom. He set her on her feet near the toilet (and seriously, the man was going to protect her against UTIs as well?) then faced the shower stall, turning on the water.

"I'm going to get you some hot cocoa," he murmured, starting for the door.

Panic.

Now he was going to leave, or worse, say this had all been a mistake—

"Rafe?"

His eyes held hers. "I'm not going anywhere." A crooked smile. "Well, I'm going to the kitchen, but I'll be back, okay?"

Her breath shuddered out of her. "Okay," she whispered.

She did her thing then wrapped up her hair and stepped into the warm steam of the shower, letting the water stream over her, not really bothering to do anything but just stand there and enjoy the heat.

A *clink* drawing her focus, and she saw Rafe, still buck naked, setting a mug on the counter.

He turned, met her eyes through the glass.

And she found herself holding her breath.

Then releasing it as he strode toward her, opened the door, and stepped into the shower with her. His hand slid down her spine, turned her to face him, his emerald gaze locking with hers. "One night," he whispered.

"One night," she agreed.

Heat in his gaze, his cock hardening and pressing into her stomach. Then...they both moved at once, and it was...effortless.

He seemed to know exactly where to put his hands to drive her absolutely wild.

She knew instinctually where to touch him that had him

groaning and shaking, his grip tightening on her, his kisses growing more and more desperate until he was lifting her up, the tiles a cold shock on her back, but only for a second.

Because then he was inside.

Her head plunked back, and he slipped a hand in between her skull and the tiles, stopping her from hurting herself, protecting her even as pleasure sucked her under.

He moved.

She moved.

They came together in a rhythm that was jerky and inelegant, filled with the sounds of water and skin sticking together, with the slick noise of desire, of his groans rumbling up in his throat, her heart pounding, his name an epithet on her tongue.

And when the pleasure had been wrung out of her, when he'd come apart, his forehead resting on her shoulder, his breath coming in rapid gusts, his body shaking from the exertion, but still he rallied himself to soap her up, to turn off the water and dry her gently, then tucked her under the covers, handed her the mug of cocoa and turned on *Die Hard* she knew...*knew* that this one night was going to absolutely destroy her.

The sounds of gunfire woke her up.

She stretched, body deliciously sore, feeling like she'd run a marathon, but one that actually made her feel great (and minus the runners' shits).

Wincing, thinking that was probably the wrong thought to have when she was naked and had just had the best sex of her life, and was still in Rafe's arms.

It wasn't night.

Their night was over.

But...he was still in her bed.

And it was all she could do to smother the hope in her heart.

One night. One. Night. This was...just a continuation of that one night.

His arms tightened, his nose was in her throat, and he inhaled deeply, pelvis rocking against hers. A hand snaking down, fingers slipping between her thighs, his lips pressing to her neck, and then he was rolling her to her stomach, lifting her up onto her knees.

A kiss on the back of her neck, drifting down along her spine. On one cheek and then the other.

She jumped when his teeth met flesh, when his fingers fluttered over her clit.

She gasped. "Rafe."

"Cor," he murmured, stroking through her folds, the head of his cock pressing into her. "Tell me you're ready."

She was ready, damned ready.

She nodded.

He thrust home.

"Fuck," she hissed.

"Too much?" he rumbled, sliding a hand down her spine, pulling out slowly, until just the head of him was inside her.

She shook her head. "No, baby."

And then there was no more talking, his hips flexing, his cock moving deep inside her. A slow drive forward, an even slower withdrawal. He fucked her like he had an eternity to drive her up and over the edge, to be inside her, to coax her to orgasm. Then when she was getting close, he froze, flipped her onto her back, rocking deep and slow until she felt like she was going to come apart at the seams.

"Wait, baby," he whispered.

She pressed her head back into her pillows. "Rafe, I need—"

A jerk of movement, him rolling them so she was on top, and then coaxing her into that final sprint. Slow and steady gone. It was fast and intense and—

"*Oh God,*" she moaned.

It was there. Right there.

Then she was over, Rafe's big hands clamped onto her waist guiding her through, guiding *him* through as wave after wave of pleasure hit her, leaving her sprawled across his chest like a limp noodle, and maybe *that* was the best sex of her life.

It hadn't been the furious coupling of the shower, nor the snap of control roughness after her date.

It was slow, steady, meaningful.

That tendril of hope blossomed inside her. She shouldn't have allowed it to. She knew that, knew that Rafe would never truly accept this change in their relationship. Not when he was supposed to protect her. Not when it would mean choosing her over her brothers.

Wyatt...fuck, he would freak out.

Asher...he wanted to pretend she didn't have a vagina, or if she did, it was safely ensconced behind a chastity belt.

Jeremy was the worst.

But Rome, Eli, and Rowan were just as bad when it came to the men she dated.

But maybe...maybe it would be different if it were Rafe.

He was a good guy. He was one of them. He—

A knock on the front door.

The heavy pounding knock of one of her brothers, followed by the worst sound in all the world—a key scraping in the lock.

Followed by an *even worse* sound.

Her brothers' voices in the hall.

One second, she was sprawled on Rafe, his warm arms around her, his hand tracing lightly up and down her back. The next she was dumped onto the mattress, her robe chucked onto her chest.

"Get dressed," he hissed as Jeremy's voice echoed up the stairs.

"Cora! You'd better be awake! It's Hike Day."

Hike. Day.

Fuck her life.

She scrambled into the robe, tying it securely at the same time as Rafe disappeared into the bathroom, his clothes bundled into his arms.

And then...they descended.

Jeremy popping his head in first, his expression tightening when he saw she wasn't dressed. "You forgot?"

She slung a hand on her hip, tried to pretend there wasn't a naked man in her bathroom. "You mean, did I forget the event I swore I would never *ever* go on again after the last time that you guys dragged me on a six-mile hike without even knowing the path you were supposed to be taking?"

"Meh," he said, shoving her arm to the side and sweeping her into a tight hug.

"Paths are for pussies," Wyatt, her second oldest (by a few minutes anyway, but definitely her tallest brother) declared, sweeping into her bedroom and dislodging Jeremy so he could steal a hug.

Then her room was invaded by Asher and Eli, who nearly knocked her over with the exuberance of their hugs (and thank God she managed to keep her feet because she was naked under the robe). Rowan and Rome were a little quieter, but then again four had come before them, and as Cora knew intimately, there was only so much air available.

And noise their ears could take.

"Sorry, peanut," Rome said, when he hugged her. "I tried to convince them to leave you out of it."

"Let me guess," she muttered, "you were outvoted, four to two, with you and Rowan being the only two voices of reason."

He pulled back, bopped her on the nose. "Got it in one."

"Look, guys," she said when she'd finished hugging Rowan, and because she needed to get them out of her room before something disastrous happened, like one of the big lugs needed to use the bathroom or something. "I'll go on the damned hike, but I need to shower first, and I need Asher to make me his oat—"

A crash in the bathroom.

"—meal," she finished, clearing her throat, hoping that her voice had drowned out the noise.

Except, six gazes had turned from her, had focused on the door to the bathroom.

Tension filled her bedroom.

She opened her mouth to say *something*, maybe to scream bloody murder about there being a spider—that had worked when she'd been a teenager—but Jeremy whipped toward her, eyes flashing as his gaze drifted from her (presumably taking in her short robe cinched tight) over her shoulder (more presuming, since he was staring in the direction of her very mussed bed). "Do you have a man in there?"

Oh, fuck.

But she was Cora Hutchins.

She'd dealt with these idiots for thirty years—and she was *thirty years old*, dammit! If she had a man in there, it was her prerogative.

"I'm a grown woman—" Or really, a *groan* one again, because Jeremy ignored her, walking toward the bathroom and reaching for the doorknob. "I can make my own—"

The door opened.

Fuck. Her. Life.

Eighteen

Rafe

The door whipped open, but he was ready.

Even though his heart was fucking racing and his palms were sweaty and he was mentally spiraling.

Disaster.

Disaster.

So fucking stupid.

The best night of his life and the worst morning...because he wouldn't ever have her again.

"What the fuck, man?"

Jeremy. Of course, it was his best friend. And, of course, his other best friend was on his heels. Wyatt's eyebrows slashing down, fury on his face.

Time to play it cool.

Even though his dick was still drying from being inside *their sister.*

He rolled his eyes. "One of you fuckers want to fix the showerhead?" he asked, stepping out of the stall and holding the piece he'd unscrewed.

This being after he'd pulled on his clothes.

Pants. Shirt. Jeans. Two shoes. Two socks. No underwear. Because he hadn't had time to find it, and he was praying that Cora's brothers didn't accidentally spot it.

Jeremy's face relaxed.

Wyatt watched him closely. "Why didn't you come out when you heard us?"

"Because I was elbow deep in showerhead?" he asked, setting it on the counter and drawing his friend into a slapping hug that made him feel both at home and like total shit, all at the same time.

Jeremy slung an arm around Cora's shoulders. "Told you it would be a perk to have a contractor staying with you." He glanced at Rafe. "Chase off any assholes?"

Cora glared. "I'm a grown woman, I can chase off my own—"

"One," he said, knowing that he was one of the assholes that should be chased off, either by Cora herself or her brothers, or probably both.

The things he'd done to her...

The things she'd done to him...

His cock twitched and...

Asshole.

Jeremy grinned, kissed the top of Cora's head. "Get dressed," he ordered, shoving her into the bedroom. The hem of her robe dancing around the tops of her thighs reminded Rafe of...*too much*. He tore his gaze away.

Not going there.

Not ever again.

"What's wrong with it?"

He frowned. "What?"

Wyatt nodded at the showerhead he'd set on the counter. "What's wrong with the showerhead?"

Rafę froze, knowing he should have an easy excuse, but

unable to come up with one.

The silence stretched, too damned far, too damn dangerously.

"It's not spraying right," Cora said, having righted herself after the shove. She stood in the doorway, looking sick, but determined, probably very similar to his own expression. The sick part, anyway.

Because the only thing he was determined about was getting the fuck out of this house and away from Cora's brothers, from his friends, until he got his head on straight...and found a new place to stay.

Clearly, this could not go on.

A breath as he pushed by Wyatt. "Did I hear something about oatmeal?" he asked. "You fuckers can cook me breakfast while I soak this showerhead in vinegar and baking soda."

He strode from the room, weaving his way through a sextuplet of men who would die for the woman among them, who would cheerfully murder him if they'd known he had just finished enjoying himself with their sister when they barged into her house.

He did it pretending that nothing had changed.

He did *it*, casually nudging his missing underwear under the bed on the way out.

"I'm so going to change the locks on you assholes," Cora grumbled from ahead of him, her ass swaying as she climbed the incline on the six-mile hike Rowan had picked for them.

For *them*.

Yup. Them including Rafe, even though he'd tried to get out of it.

Because as much as Cora protested about their pushiness,

Rafe wasn't immune, even though he'd attempted the excuse of needing to work.

They'd strong-armed him into the hike.

And now...now he was in hell.

And the self-flagellation was real. He'd been in an inner spiral of panic and disgust, one that kept being sparked because now that he'd had Cora, he couldn't look at her and not see the rich brown skin he'd kissed, breasts he'd had in his hands, nipples he'd tasted, a pussy he'd had on his tongue.

And he was with her brothers.

Which then meant the cycle started right back up again.

So, the self-punishment was real.

Ceaseless.

God, he had to think about something, *anything* aside from the way it had felt to cup Cora's hips and thrust deep inside her hot, wet puss—

"You good?"

He nearly skidded off the trail, and considering it was a hill on one side and a sharp precipice on the other (anyone want to guess which side he nearly toppled off?) there were a few good seconds there where his life flashed before his eyes.

He didn't hate that the last night of his life had been spent with Cora.

Which...presented a problem.

A hand gripped his arm—a hand that belonged to Wyatt. "You good?" he asked, studying Rafe closely.

Rafe cleared his throat. "I'm fine."

"You're not yourself."

He wasn't.

Because he'd *fucked their sister!*

"Yeah," he said, "my mind is on my new projects. Got a busy schedule coming up, and it's going to mean a lot of travel between here and L.A. until the job down there is complete."

"That sucks, man." Wyatt nodded ahead and they moved to

catch up, Rafe thankful they were at the back of the pack and the other brothers couldn't give him too much shit about his near-death experience.

"Still planning on moving up here?" Wyatt asked.

Rafe nodded. "Yeah, that's another thing. The L.A. job is the last one, and then we're going to have two years of busting our asses until we finish our current contracts. So, I need to find some time to find a place to buy or rent, considering that I can't stay in Cora's spare room forever."

"She wouldn't mind."

Laughter in his chest. "You've either lost it, or you don't know your sister. She barely let me stay *this* time."

"Meh. Cora's bark is worse than her bite. She always relents."

That reminded him of what Teresa had said, about the warning she'd given. "Maybe, Wy," he agreed. "But at some point, she's going to be done relenting and you guys might actually end up with more problems than her dating a guy you don't approve of."

Furrows in Wyatt's brows. "What the fuck are you talking about? Did Cora say something? Is she dating—"

Rafe shook his head. "You know I'm a lifelong member of the Protect Cora fan club, but I'm just saying that she's a grown-up, and she's going to start resenting the interference in her life at some point." A beat. "If she hasn't already."

The grooves on his forehead were deep. "Did she say something?"

"No." He shook his head. "I just—my foreman, Teresa, mentioned something. She's got brothers, and the overprotectiveness strained their relationship."

Immediately, the worry left his face. "Well, that's Teresa. Cor's different."

"I don't—"

A cry.

Cora cried out.

And Rafe stopped thinking and spiraling and trying to make Wyatt see reason. He heard Cora was in pain, and...

He reacted.

Nineteen

Cora

One second, she was grousing about the hike and huffing and puffing as she followed Jeremy, Rome, Eli, and Rowan up the hill, and the next she was falling, seeing Asher's eyes go wide in horror.

He'd nudged her, a playful brotherly push, telling her to stop her complaining.

But she'd been between strides, and the push was ill-timed.

She caught her foot on a tree root...and tripped.

Fell sideways.

Right over the edge of the path.

Her hip hit something hard—a rock, another root—and then she was sliding, rolling. Pain through her temple, her cheek as she was caught by a branch.

She heard a shout, but she didn't know which of the males it belonged to.

Not when she was scrabbling, nails breaking as she tried to claw at the hillside, trying to slow her descent.

But it was all loose rocks and leaves and crumbling dirt and—

A jarring pain shooting up her back.

It took a moment for her to realize that she'd come to a halt, mostly because rocks and dirt, leaves and sticks kept sliding by her for long moments.

She lifted a hand, saw it was covered with blood, deep gouges dug into her palm, several of her nails broken, blood seeping. Then she tried to move.

Everything hurt.

Her toes in her boots. Her ankles, calves, shins. Her knees felt like they'd had a run-in with a rototiller. Her thighs and ass were on fire. Her back was oozing. Her arms on fire. Her face...it felt like her nose might be broken.

"Fuck," she hissed, trying to lift her head then promptly freezing and lying back down.

"Cora!"

Movement above her, rocks and dirt, leaves and sticks tumbling down again, bumping into her, creating a whole new net of pain as they collided with her.

"I'm okay," she whispered.

"Cora!"

"I'm okay," she managed to say a little louder.

"Cora, fuck. Cora, baby." Rafe skidded to a halt next to her, nearly going over the edge himself, having to grip the trunk of the tree to stop himself. "Shit." He extended a hand toward her, pulled back before he touched her. "*Fuck.* Baby, oh my God."

"I'm okay," she whispered again. "I just—"

More rocks and sticks, dirt and leaves began coming down again.

Rafe lurched forward, blocking the flurry, covering her body with his own, somehow without smushing her. "Stop!" he yelled. "You're knocking shit down onto Cora."

Curses, but the flurry stopped.

"Is she okay?" Jeremy called.

"I'm fine," she called back...and winced because her ribs, her ribs didn't like it when she raised the volume of her voice.

"She's not fine," Rafe yelled. "Get the first aid kit ready. I'll get her up to you."

She shifted her leg, stifled a pained groan.

"Stop moving," Rafe ordered, turning to face her.

She ignored him, kept going until she managed to get both of her legs on the same side of the tree. A hiss of air when she put her hand beneath her, but before her arm gave out and she collapsed back down to the ground, Rafe's arms were around her.

"Stop," he ordered.

Her teeth clinked together, sending a bolt of pain along her jaw. "I'm—"

"You're not *fine*," he growled. "You're hurting and bleeding from a dozen different places. It's a god damn miracle you're conscious, and I'm not even sure you don't have broken bones or a fucking skull fracture."

Miserably, she lifted a hand to her head, trying to smother her wince at the movement. "Don't yell at me."

"Then don't fall off a fucking cliff," he snapped, gently lifting her up.

She cried out.

She *hated* that she'd cried out, but it had just slipped out.

Rafe cursed. "I'm sorry, baby."

Concentrating on breathing, it took her a long minute to be able to speak without crying. "It's not your fault."

"Yeah, it's fucking Asher's fault," he muttered. "And I'm going to take care of *him* later."

He shifted her, and the gentle movement had her teeth clenching, had pain shooting along her jaw again, had fire shooting through her torso. Fuck, that really hurt. She didn't know how she was going to stand being carried up this hill.

All she knew was that she wasn't going to be able to walk up it.

So, she *had* to stand it.

"I'm sorry in advance for this, baby," he warned, arms tightening slightly. "But I've got to get you up this hill."

"Just do it," she ordered.

Rafe's eyes hit hers. They were gentle, with deep regret in their depths. "Sorry, baby," he whispered.

"It's—"

But the rest of her words were cut off on a pained breath.

Because he was moving up the hill, arms wrapped tightly around her as he climbed the slope. His body pitched forward so he wouldn't fall. Occasionally releasing one arm so he could grab onto a root or rock to heft them higher.

All of it hurt.

Every jar and movement. Every heft and shift of his grip.

They were agony.

But then there were more arms around them, hands grabbing onto Rafe as they hauled them up and over the edge.

"Put her down over here," Jeremy ordered.

Rafe carried her across the trail, set her gently on a pile of sweatshirts.

The moment his hands were off her body, he stood, spinning and cold-cocking Asher.

She gasped. Then whimpered.

"Save that shit for later," Jeremy snapped, and then he was bending over her, hands fluttering like he didn't know how to touch her without hurting her. And he probably couldn't. As previously established, she hurt everywhere. "Fuck, Cor, you're a mess," he said gently.

"I'm fine. Just bandage up the worst of the cuts and wrap my ribs so we can get out of here."

His eyes flared when she said ribs, but he didn't get up and punch Asher in the face again like she half expected. Instead, he sucked in a breath, released it slowly. Then he began cleaning the worst of the wounds, his jaw clenching so tightly that she was worried he was going to crack a tooth. He startled slightly when Rafe knelt beside them, shaking out his fist. His fingers were gentle when he slowly pulled up the hem of her shirt, probing gently at her ribs.

"You'll need an X-ray," he said softly.

Movement at her feet, Rowan's voice terse as it reached her ears. "And here." Fingers loosened the laces, gently tugged off the boot. "It's already swelling."

Rome crouched at her other side, grabbed a wipe, and began cleaning her face. "Maybe a CT Scan."

If she weren't hurting so much, she'd be losing her shit. Four of them hovering over her, three others bare feet away.

But for the moment, she just wanted to lie there long enough to summon the energy to get up and make her way back to the car. She knew they'd barely made it a mile on the trail, but that mile back was going to be hell.

So, she didn't freak out about the hovering.

She closed her eyes, rallied her strength, and vowed, "I'm never fucking hiking again."

"I swear to fuck," she growled as they argued about who was going to carry her into the house, "if all of you don't back the fuck up and let me hobble my ass into the house..."

Asher was feeling guilty and was being over-the-top protective.

Jeremy was the oldest, needed to feel in control.

Rowan and Rome were hanging back, but they'd both offered to help.

Wyatt had already moved to the door, had it wide open.

And Eli was trying to make the case that he was the biggest, the strongest, so *obviously,* he should be carrying her into the house.

Then suddenly, her brothers were pushed away, and Rafe was there.

"Arms on my shoulders, baby," he whispered in her ear, leaning close and crouching down so that she could grab on. "One. Two. *Three.*"

Her teeth clenched, but she managed to hold back her groan of pain.

"Easy now, baby," he whispered. "Okay?"

She swallowed hard. "Okay."

Then they began walking into her place, slower than a granny using a walker, and probably more painfully.

Definitely more painfully.

"Brace," Rafe said.

He barely gave her the time to do that before he was bending slightly, scooping her up into his arms. She gasped, the pain still there, but it wasn't the worst sort, not when he was moving so gently, holding her so carefully.

And it was a hell of a lot better than the slow, painful trudge up her front walk with Rafe holding her, carrying her up the stairs and into her house. Then she was on the second story, moving into her bedroom, and he was pausing, waiting for Jeremy to pull back the covers before he set her gently onto the mattress.

Her shoes off.

"Let me get you some pajamas," he said softly, kneeling at the edge of the mattress and squeezing her wrist lightly, one of the few spots on her that wasn't scraped to shit.

"On it already," Rowan said. "Why don't you all step out and I'll help her?"

There was some shuffling, some movement that told her

they'd all followed Rafe into her bedroom, and she knew they were worried, so she did her best to smile even though she was ready for a pain pill and to sleep for a hundred years.

"I called Kate," Rafe said. "She, Stef, Kels, and Heidi will be here in the morning. I told her not to come tonight." He pulled a bottle of pain pills from her pocket, shook out one and handed it to her. A glass—from Eli—appeared at his elbow, and he helped her sit up enough to swallow the pill. "Figured you'd just want to sleep," he said once he'd helped her lie down again.

She nodded. "Thanks," she whispered.

"Anything for you." He stood, started for the door.

"Rafe?"

He stopped. "Yeah, honey?"

Her heart skipped a beat, but she kept her voice neutral. "I..." Her gaze drifted around the room, to her brothers stationed like sentinels. "I...just...thanks."

A nod. Then he was gone, and everyone but Asher and Rowen following him. Rowen took one look at his brother, set the pajamas on the bed, and said softly, "I'll let Asher help you."

"Okay," she whispered.

"Rest easy, sweetheart," Rowan murmured. "I'll check on you later."

Big, annoying, protective lug. No. *Lugs.* Because they were also *her* big, annoying protective lugs. "I love you," she said.

"Love you too, Cor." He squeezed her ankle—the uninjured one—then disappeared into the hall behind the rest of the lugs.

And that left Asher.

Whose eyes were swollen. Both of them. And not from crying.

She winced.

He hurried over, hands flapping. "What is it? What's the matter? I can—"

She reached for his hand, caught it, and tugged him lightly

toward her. "Your face." Her lips twitched. "I don't mean that as a bad sister joke. Your eyes. I-I'm sorry Rafe and Jeremy punched you."

He crouched down next to her, head hanging. "I deserved it."

"No, honey"—a squeeze—"you didn't. We were messing around, and it was an accident." A shitty one, but still an accident.

Gently, he tugged out of her hold, hands clenching into fists. "I pushed you off a fucking cliff, Cor."

He had.

He really had.

And for some fucking reason—perhaps the pain pill they'd given her in the hospital joining with the one that Rafe had just given her, with the floating feeling just beginning to creep in and soften the edges of her hurt—she found that funny. She let out a giggle, clutching at her ribs because, Christ, that hurt, even with that pleasant fog just beginning to drift in. "You *did*," she said, tears forming at the corners of her eyes, more giggles bursting out of her in little cascades of pain. "Oh my God, you so totally did. Mom is going to *kill* you."

His face went comically scared, and her laughter got louder and slightly more painful.

But that was okay because after a few moments, he began chuckling softly, the guilt abated—slightly, she figured, since if *she* had pushed someone off a cliff, she definitely would be feeling real guilt, and feeling it for a good long while.

Still, his expression eased, and he laughed with her, agreeing, "Mom definitely is going to kill me."

She loved the big lug, especially because he took her teasing on the chin, and she knew that while the guilt might not ever completely go away, it *would* get better.

Because they had to laugh about it.

That was what Hutchinses did.

They cried, they laughed, they moved on.

Then they brought up the story at every family dinner, every holiday, every birthday...*forever*.

Twenty

Rafe

He hadn't slept the night before.

By the time they'd gotten home from the hospital, and he'd managed to calm down Jeremy and Wyatt and the others—with beer and DoorDashed BBQ—Asher had come downstairs, announcing that she was asleep.

The guys had stayed late, taking turns checking on Cora until he'd managed to send them home, reminding them her friends would be there in the morning, and that he could cover her for the few hours remaining between then and when they would show up.

So, by three in the morning, the Hutchins clan had gone off to get some rest, and he had sat in Cora's bedroom, back against the wall by the door, watching her sleep, unable to close his own eyes.

Because he couldn't stop thinking about that moment he'd seen Cora go over the edge.

Her eyes going wide, a scream piercing the air.

Asher frozen in horror, arm outstretched.

He didn't remember moving, just suddenly, he was next to her, and she was bleeding and hurt and—

"Fuck," he whispered, shoving a hand through his hair.

He knew that would be a nightmare he would have for the rest of his life.

Now, he was trying not to hover. Cora was still in bed. Her crew had arrived with bags in hand and what he assumed were the proper accoutrements for a friend who'd fallen down a fucking cliffside. Now there was chatter and quiet laughter, and he knew they'd take care of her.

But he couldn't stop himself from taking care of her either.

Which was why he was hovering in the hall, a cup of cocoa in hand, her bottle of pain pills in the other, and knowing he could have lost her.

Could *still* lose her in so many ways.

If they—

He shook his head, not willing to go there. Not right then. There would be plenty of time for guilt later.

Now, she needed her pills.

Cautiously, he stepped into the doorway, knocked on the door, the pills rattling in the container.

Five female heads turned in his direction.

Cora was still in her pajamas, the blankets folded around her middle.

She looked tired, like she was feeling worse than the night before, and he suspected that the next couple of days would be the worst, as far as the aches and pains went.

And that made sense.

Two bruised ribs. A sprained ankle. Three cuts that had required a total of twelve stitches. Glue on her temple and the side of her scalp.

She was banged up.

She was hurting.

He hated that.

So even though he should probably take the time to back up and erect some distance between them, he couldn't. He just... couldn't.

He walked to the bed, hovered by the edge since there wasn't room to sit on the edge, not with her friends perched on top of it, food and books and beauty products spread between them. Kate was dabbing some sort of cream on Cora's scabs. Heidi was smoothing an oil into the ends of Cora's hair, and Stef was gingerly painting Cora's toes. Kels was next to Cora, pillows propped up behind them both, and had been showing her something on a tablet.

"Sorry to interrupt the spa party."

Stef smiled up at him. "Please, interrupt," she said on a laugh. "Save Cora from my horrible pedicure."

"I think it looks nice," Kate said.

He glanced at Cora's toes, knew that generally a pedicure meant keeping polish on the nails and not the toes, but kept that comment to himself.

Stef bit her lip, tightened the lid on the nail polish. "I just know when I broke my ankle, I liked my toes to look pretty."

"Stef?" Cora asked.

Her friend shifted her gaze to Cora's.

"Thanks," Cora said.

His heart squeezed, lungs going tight. Good friends. Good people. And Cora, the girl he'd grown up protecting and loving as a sister, had become such a good *woman*.

He cleared his throat. "I just have your pain pills," he said softly. "And some hot cocoa." He felt the women's gazes on him when he put the mug on her nightstand, shook out a couple of pills and handed them to her.

Then watched, probably creepily, while she took them.

After she was done, he had a hard time leaving the room, but he forced himself to turn around, to walk into the hall.

But the whole time he did so, he felt like he'd left part of himself in that bed.

"Hey."

He glanced up from his laptop, saw Kate standing in the living room.

The rest of the women had gone home an hour earlier, but Kate had insisted on staying and baking Cora's favorite chocolate chunk cookies before Jaime came to pick her up. She winced and rubbed her belly.

"Hey," he said, closing the laptop and standing up. "Is everything okay?"

Her brows pulled together. "You mean because I'm eight million years pregnant?"

More like eight and a half months, at least that's what he thought based on the dinner conversation the previous week. "Yes, Kate. Because of that. Is the baby coming?" he asked. "Because I think Cora would be pissed if you ruined her rug by having a baby on it. I'm not even allowed to wear my shoes on it."

She laughed then broke off and winced again, rubbed her belly again.

And he had to admit, he might have been joking, but all the wincing and the belly-rubbing had him more than a little freaked out. He hustled over to her at the same time as he pulled out his phone. He was going to call Jaime—

A hand covered his.

"It's fine," she said. "Just the baby trying to get comfortable when there's not a lot of room in here."

Yeah, that didn't exactly make him feel better.

Because less room meant that baby was almost done being cooked.

Which meant it might come out.

While he was here.

A nudge. "Sit down," Kate ordered. "I'll get you a cookie, and..." His ass hit the couch and then his eyes opened, connected with hers. "I...um...I'm guessing this is yours, and that you...um...don't...um...want Cor's brothers to accidentally find it."

"I—"

Fuck.

He took it, shoved it in his pocket. "Right. I—"

She turned around and disappeared into the kitchen.

"Right," he whispered again.

His underwear. How the fuck could he have forgotten—

"Here."

Kate was back and shoving a half dozen cookies at him, along with a beer. When he frowned at the combo, she sank down next to him, munching on her own stack of cookies. "Jaime says it's a weird but good combination."

Since the cookies smelled delicious and the beer was cold, he shut up and started eating and drinking.

Learning that the combination *was* good.

Learning that the conversation was going to bring up a bunch of *not* good.

"It's in the way you look at her."

His eyes shot to hers. "What are you talking about?"

"You love her," she whispered. "You love her with your eyes."

"I—" He shook his head. "Um, no, that's not—"

"Rafe." Just his name, said in a way that was gentle, but also threaded with steel. "Don't bullshit me," she said. "I've experienced that look plenty. I've been around you and her enough over the years to know. The look in your eyes is no longer just that of a protective brother."

He inhaled.

"It's possessive," she said. "You want her. And not like a sibling." A beat. "You want her like a man."

"That's not—"

But he stopped. Because...Kate, with her sincere brown eyes locked onto his, her caring expression holding him in place...and he couldn't lie.

But he also couldn't admit the truth.

Because of what it would mean. What it would change.

So...he just didn't say anything. Didn't agree or disagree. He just looked down at his beer, ate his cookies, tried to pretend that he wasn't watching Kate's expression change from caring to disappointed.

"I know," she said after a few minutes of eating and drinking in silence. "I know that things are complicated with Cora's brothers, but if you really love her, if you're really willing to fight for her—"

"I'm not."

Kate sucked in a breath. "If you fight for her, they will accept it. Accept you."

They wouldn't.

"I'm not going to fight for her."

"Rafe," Kate began. "I know you're—"

Heart pounding, he stood up. "You don't know anything." Her fingers caught his. "*Anything*." Not wanting to hurt her, he gently extricated himself. But after he'd rinsed his beer bottle and put it in the recycle bin, he didn't go back into the family room, didn't wait for Jamie to get there, even though it was kind of a dick move.

Instead, he bypassed the room altogether and snuck up the stairs.

And hid.

From the truth. From the reality.

From the future.

Twenty-One

Cora

She had freshly painted toes, cuts that were hurting a whole lot less thanks to Kate and her magical ointment (which, maybe Cora should have been pissed about, because it was for animals, though according to Jaime, none of the ingredients could hurt humans), and she'd slept for what felt like an eternity.

So long that her eyes were crusty.

Sighing, she rolled over and glanced at her phone, knowing that there would be a plethora of messages from Dale.

She'd given her notice, and now she was "conveniently ill."

His words.

Not hers.

And not that she was saying she wanted to be hurt and laid up in bed with a sprained ankle, two bruised ribs, stitches, cuts and scrapes and contusions all over, and miss her last two weeks of work. She wasn't a hero.

She didn't like pain, so waking up hurting like this meant that she was pretty miserable.

Not miserable enough to wish she were at work.

Who said there weren't small victories in life?

Especially if the consequence of her slide down a hillside meant she worked remotely and didn't have to deal with Dale?

She'd consider that as a win.

Now, however, as she reached for her phone, all she encountered was a naked nightstand. Her phone cord was still there, attached with a little clip she'd bought online to stop it from falling to the floor all the time.

But the part that plugged into her phone was empty.

Frowning, she gingerly sat up, holding her ribs which still hurt like hell, and though she was still cut and bruised in other places, she was happy to report that it hurt less than the day before.

Once vertical, she saw that her nightstand wasn't completely naked. There was a napkin with a few crackers and her pain pills on it, and sitting alongside that was a bottle of water.

Rafe.

All Rafe.

He'd been wrangling her friends and her brothers, popping in to check on her a few times as the day went on, and considering that the girls had been there all day, and then her brothers had come to check on her in intervals (and not all at once, descending like locusts and staying to eat the crops...of cookies Kate had made), she knew he'd been playing doorman, too.

After eating the crackers, she made short work of the pills and was debating whether or not to get out of bed and risk hobbling on her crutches by herself to the bathroom when she heard it.

Rafe's raised voice.

Frowning, she opted for the hobbling, only instead of to the bathroom, she was hobbling to the hallway, to where Rafe was standing, his back to her, one hand clenching her phone, the other in a fist at his side.

"I don't really give a fuck what *you* want, Dale," he snapped. "Your employee had a serious accident this weekend and needs time to heal. *If* she feels up to working from home in a few days—which I'm sure she will because Cora isn't the type of woman to not fulfill her responsibilities, then she will do so when she feels up to it. She will *not* do it just because you keep blowing up her phone and are acting like an asshole."

Silence.

Listening.

Then, "Did you not hear what I said about the whole *acting like an asshole* thing?"

More silence.

Then, "Nope. I guess you didn't. So, if you don't get your head out of your ass, I'll report you to your HR department, and if that goes nowhere, then I'll make sure to contact the Division of Labor and the Better Business Bureau to report your company for not allowing employees to use their sick time they've *legally earned.*"

A beat of quiet this time.

"Yeah," Rafe said. "I will. So don't fuck with me or Cora. Shut up, sit tight or that report will include a complaint on the forced overtime Cora's also been pulling." A pause. "Yeah," he said. "I will definitely go there." More silence then, "Uh-huh. My advice? Chill the fuck out, trust the employee you've hired to get the work done, and then thank your lucky stars that she's not the type of person to fuck you over. *Then* do some soul-searching, asshole, and change your management strategy. Because I don't give a fuck how good your product is, if you can't manage people correctly, you're going to crash and burn."

He went quiet again, listening.

Then he sighed. "Yeah, unfortunately, I can see that you're not going to take my advice. Cora will be in touch when she feels up to it. Good luck in the future, dick bag."

He jabbed at the phone screen, holding the cell in his fist, tightly enough that she had to wonder if he was going to break it, but then he sighed, relaxed his grip, and turned around, startling when he saw her.

"Cor?" he asked.

She smiled, heart skipping a beat for some reason.

No.

Not for some reason, but because he didn't have a shirt on, and his chest was yummy, and she'd kissed her way across it and—

She wanted him.

Not right that instant, since her ribs were aching, and she really wasn't feeling the whole hobbling around on crutches thing.

"How much did you hear?"

A shuddering breath that hurt coming out. "Of your verbal smackdown with Dale?"

He winced. "Right," he said, "so all of it."

"Most of it," she corrected. "I...thanks for standing up for me. You didn't have to."

"He called your phone a good fifty times," he muttered. "And that was before seven o'clock. You need your rest."

"Still," she said. "You didn't have to do that."

"I did." He stuck her phone in his pocket. "And now you need to get back into bed. You need your rest, Cor."

"Honey"—she reached for his hand as he came close, wobbling slightly on the crutches because she'd taken one hand off the wheel, so to speak—"I'm fine. I just—"

He lifted her up, her crutches falling to the floor.

"Rafe!"

"Bed," he repeated.

And when he got all growly and demanding and started talking about bed, she remembered their night and she...

Yeah. Hot damn. One night hadn't been nearly enough.

He stepped over the crutches, strode down the hall, and

started to deposit her on the mattress. "Wait," she said before he could release her. "I need to—" She tilted her head in the direction of the bathroom.

A flick of his gaze from her to the door. "Right," he whispered, hefting her up again and walking into the bathroom, setting her gingerly on her good foot. "Do you need—?"

"So help me God, if you ask if I need help using the toilet, we're going to have problems," she muttered. "I don't care how sweet you've been to me."

Emerald eyes on hers. "Right," he said. "I'll wait outside until you need me."

"Good plan."

Snorting, he moved from her—after he made sure she was steady on that good foot—and then left the bathroom, though she didn't miss that he didn't latch the door completely.

She did her thing—

Also, this just in, having bruised ribs did *not* make it easy to sit her ass onto the toilet. But she managed, did her business, hauled herself up, and hobbled to the sink to wash her hands, brush her teeth, and tame her hair.

Then she reached for the bathroom door.

Which barely missed her face as Rafe pushed it open.

"Jesus," he muttered, halting it an inch from her nose.

"Yeah," she grumbled. "Tell *me* about it."

His fingers brushed over her cheek. "Sorry, honey."

Ouch.

The endearment had her inhaling sharply, longing filling her, and that—shocker of shockers, that hurt her ribs.

His gaze had been on hers, but her response had him looking away, that muscle in his jaw ticking all over again.

"Come on," he said, lifting her up, carrying her, and putting her into bed. "You need anything?" he asked after he'd tucked her under the covers.

"Yeah."

He paused, glanced back at her, question in his eyes.

"Are we really just going to do this?" she asked.

That question grew.

"Just going to pretend it didn't happen?"

His expression clouded. "Cor—"

"I know," she whispered. "I know you said one night, Rafe, but...how? How do we do just one night when our night together was..." She pushed up, sucked in a breath, and just told him what had been in her heart since the night he'd first kissed her, from the moment she realized that he might be feeling a little of what she'd been feeling for ages. "It was the best I've ever had. *Ever.* And I mean *ever.* And I know you're a good guy and I've"—a breath—"and truthfully, I've had a crush on you forever. I just never thought we'd...you'd know—"

She bit her lip, struggling with the words, hoping he would say something.

But he didn't, didn't say anything. He just stared at her, his expression unfathomable.

Her heart was on a slow sink.

Just an anchor hooked into her, drawing her down and down and *down.* Until she was going to drown in those cold green eyes.

"I mean," she finally said, "was it not good?"

"*No.*"

The anchor was joined by a dozen more, yanking her under the surface of the water, the cold liquid gushing into her nose, down her throat. Choking now. Choking on hurt and despair and...maybe just the slightest bit of bitterness.

"Right," she said. "I think you need to find somewhere else to—"

"It was the best. Hands down."

She blinked, but then he was there, sitting next to her on the bed, fingers smoothing back her hair, brushing lightly over the cut there. "What?" she breathed.

"The night. The morning. Us together"—he took a breath, released it slowly—"it was...I've never felt like that, never had that, never—" He sighed and shook his head. "But I can't do this. I can't—"

Her heart had been drifting up, nearing the surface.

But his words sent her sinking again, a slow, downward drag.

"Why?" she asked.

He was still. Like a big, handsome statue.

"If it's the best and, fuck, I mean we've known each other our whole lives," she said, knowing she was blabbering. "We get along for the most part, and we know each other. You get along with my mom, with my brothers—"

"Cora."

"And it's not like I'm saying we should walk down the aisle" —though she couldn't lie and say she hadn't written about it in her diary at the ripe old age of fourteen...and fifteen...and sixteen —"I just, we could see how things go and—"

"*Cora*."

"And my brothers love you. You'd be the first man they couldn't run off and—"

His eyes slid closed. "Honey," he whispered. His forehead rested on hers. "Honey," he said again.

"Just try, baby," she murmured. "We can just try. No expectations, just...us."

She watched his nostrils flare as he inhaled. "I—we could—"

"What the *fuck?*"

Rafe stiffened and straightened, head jerking as he looked over his shoulder.

Jeremy was there, expression thunderous.

"What. The. Fuck?" he snapped. "What are you doing to my sister?"

Fucking Jeremy.

Rafe had hopped to his feet like a goddamned whack-a-mole, his face going pale. He looked like he'd committed the most grievous of crimes...and maybe according to the bro code, he had.

Which was why she gave him the out.

"Chill, Jeremy," she snapped before her brother freaked out even more completely. "He was checking my stitches. A piece of my hair got stuck in one of them, and I was worried that it got pulled out."

Rafe had turned back to face her, and the relief in his eyes made her sick.

God, what was she doing?

He didn't want her or didn't want her enough to deal with her brothers, so really that was the same thing.

She'd all but thrown herself at him, and he...

Didn't want her enough.

So...the sex was incredible, their night was one that might ruin her for all future men, but...he wasn't going to take a chance on her. So, she wasn't going to do this, wasn't going to draw it out, to make herself feel like a reject over and over again.

He'd done it with the kiss.

He'd done it when her brothers had shown up announced.

He'd done it just now.

So now it was three times that he'd made her feel like crap.

Three times was three times too many.

She was Cora Fucking Hutchins. She didn't get her heart trampled by men. She didn't sit and feel hurt and sorry for herself just because she wasn't woman enough for a man.

Wasn't enough for Rafe.

So, fuck him.

And fuck her brothers for that matter. It was beyond time for them to stop interfering in her life. She'd given them far too much leeway in her life, hadn't set boundaries or had set them and let them keep busting right through them. But she'd had enough.

Of them.

Of Rafe.

A free place to stay. A free fuck.

But not worth fighting for. Not worth standing up to her brothers for.

Not worth *enough.*

So...enough.

Rafe could just get the fuck out of her place, and her brothers could as well.

She was changing the fucking locks—and getting one of those automatic locks where she could give (or revoke) a code at will.

Seemingly satisfied, Jeremy turned to Rafe. "How is she this morning?"

Like Cora wasn't *right there.* Conscious and wholly capable of sharing about her own health.

"I'm fine," she said before Rafe could answer for her.

Which seemed to bounce off the walls and through the space, remaining totally unheard.

And seriously? What. The. Fuck?

"She's stiff and still can't put weight on the ankle, but I think overall a little better."

She tried again. "I'm—"

"And the ribs?"

"Still very tender from what I can—"

"Out!"

It was a yell, so loud and intense she practically scared herself. But it had the desired effect. Both Rafe and Jeremy turned to her.

"What's the matter?

A snapped out question from her brother...and seriously, the wrong thing to say. What was the matter? *The matter?*

"You mean despite the fact that I've let you assholes butt into my life for too fucking long?"

Their brows lifted, almost in unison. Then Asher popped

his head in, followed by Wyatt. And she knew—*knew*—that the rest of them were just down the hall, ready to invade and take charge, and the worst fucking part of that was that *she* had allowed it.

And that just pissed her off more.

"It's my fucking life," she snapped. "My life, and I swear to God, I need you all to back off and let me live it."

"Cor—" Jeremy began in a condescending tone.

"No! You need to stop. I didn't even *want* to hike, and now I'm laid up in bed with bruised ribs, stitches, and a sprained fucking ankle. I didn't want you to run off my boyfriend or interfere with my job"—she glared at Rafe—"I don't want you to just show up at my place without calling or texting first. I don't want you to act like I'm still six years old and need to be looked after! I'm a grown woman with my own life, and you are only in it because I allow you to be—"

"Cora, honey," Rafe began.

She jabbed a finger in his direction. "No," she snapped. "You don't get to have an opinion either."

He reared back.

Wyatt opened his mouth.

Her finger went in his direction. "Neither do you!"

"You're our sister—"

"I know!" She tossed her hands in the air. "Your baby sister who never pushes back, but I'm done. *Done!* D.O.N.E. *Done!*" The last she punctuated with another finger jab. But apparently it was too vigorous because pain shot down her side and the rest of her words were cut off on a gasp.

Rafe started toward her. "Cora—"

"Don't," she yelled.

"And I think it's time for you all to go."

Her eyes shot to the door, seeing Heidi and Kate pushing their way in through the mass of her brothers, Heidi's calm but firm words having her brothers turning in her direction.

"But—" Jeremy began.

Kate's expression turned mulish. "That wasn't a request, Jeremy Hutchins. It was an order. Cora has had enough, and you guys are messing up her recovery."

Heidi nodded. "So you need to go, and you need to stop smothering her."

"And not come back until she tells you she's ready," added Kate.

Collectively, her brothers began to shake their heads, and Cora braced for a refusal.

But then, surprisingly, Rafe took her side.

"We all need to go," he said. "Well, all of us except Heidi and Kate."

"But—" Jeremy began.

"Wyatt?" he said, lifting his eyebrows pointedly.

Wyatt's expression was hard, but after Rafe had held his eyes for a few seconds, he blew out a breath and sighed. "They're right." The words were begrudging. "We need to go."

"I—"

"Jer."

Her brother stopped, stared at Wyatt.

And then he sighed as well. "Right," he said. "We'll go." With that, he crossed to her, kissed her cheek, and left the room, her brothers saying their goodbyes and doing the same. Kate and Heidi followed them out, and she could kiss them for making sure they left.

But Rafe didn't follow them.

"Cora."

Twenty-Two

Rafe

His heart squeezed tight when she turned away from him, her eyes closing.

"Honey," he said again.

Those eyes shot open. "No," she said, and the hurt threaded through her voice tore him to shreds. "No, you don't get to call me that."

"You know why we can't—"

"I know why you *think* we can't." Vulnerability and pain and tears in the corners of her eyes. "But what you need to understand is that every time you say that we can't be together because you don't want to mess up things with them, don't want to lose them, what you're actually saying is that I'm not worth enough to take that risk."

His heart had moved beyond squeezes. Now the organ had been tossed into a blender and the puree button had been pushed. She didn't understand. He cared for her, loved her, but he felt so much of both emotions and it was all tangled up with his past. He'd worked so hard to be part of the family, tried so hard to be a Hutchins.

What if he fucked it all up?

What if they looked at him like his father had and—

"You keeping your distance, saying you want me, but that want isn't enough means that *I'm* not enough."

Oh, fuck. That was the last thing he ever wanted her to feel. *Ever.* "It's not like—"

"Cut the bullshit. It's *exactly* like that. You're attracted to me. You want me. But not enough to stand up to my brothers. Not enough to tell them the truth and bear whatever fallout might come from it."

The worst part?

He couldn't deny that it was the truth. He wanted Cora. From the moment he'd kissed her, everything had changed. He couldn't think of anything else, of *anyone* else, hadn't been able to stop wanting and needing her. He'd been pretending that his living at her place was because of her brothers, but he knew it was because of *him*.

Because he hadn't wanted to leave Cora.

Because he wanted her.

Just...not—

"I get that I'm not enough," she said. "And that's the fucking truth. So, you can play at being protective, but I know it's a fucking joke because the one you're actually protecting is *you.*"

"Women," Jeremy said, drunk as hell, but still drinking.

They all were.

Rafe included.

Rafe *especially*.

He lifted his beer to his lips, taking another long swallow.

This was beer...five...six...fuck, he'd lost count. All he knew was the edges of Wyatt's house were looking fuzzy and every single one of Cora's brothers were as drunk as he was.

Because Cora had kicked them out.

Because—at least for him—Cora had flayed him to the very core with her words.

No. With the truth.

Because what she had said was true, and the moment he'd realized that was the moment she had told him off, he had realized she was right.

He was protecting himself.

Because he was scared of being alone again.

Scared of not being enough, and in all that fear he'd allowed to rule him, he'd made Cora feel like *she* wasn't enough.

He'd hurt her.

He'd hadn't protected her heart.

He'd stomped on it, and then thrown it in the blender alongside his.

"Can't live with 'em," Rowen muttered.

"Shut up," Wyatt said, turning to Rafe. "He warned me." A nod at Rafe. "I didn't think that it was a real possibility."

"What'd you tell Wyatt?"

Jeremy's eyes locked onto Rafe's.

"My friend, Teresa, warned me this might happen. That we were overstepping and might burn some bridges. I mentioned it to Wyatt because, staying at her place, I've seen her frustrated. I thought it might be something that could happen at some point. I just didn't—" He sighed, drank deeply. "I guess I didn't think it would really happen."

"Fuck," Rome said. "Yeah, who would? We've always been there for her."

"Kind of feels a little ungrateful," Eli muttered. "I mean, it's not like we did anything really bad."

Asher snorted. "Except, push her off a fucking cliff."

Rafe clapped him on the back. "Accident, man. Remember?"

Asher's gaze dropped to his hands, to the bottle clenched between them. "Yeah," he hissed. "I remember." But the anger was self-directed. They all knew it, and though tempers had exploded on the trail, the fury had passed, and it would never be as intense as Asher's own at himself.

Because he'd hurt Cora.

And they'd all vowed that would never happen.

She'd missed out on a lot. She didn't have the same memories of Tom, of the great father he'd been. She'd missed out on the fun vacations, the new clothes, the big birthday parties. They'd been a family of seven on a single mother's salary.

And the only memories she had of that time were fuzzy and more feeling-based than something actually concrete.

Rafe wasn't even part of the family, and he had memories of Tom, of Mr. Hutchins.

And they were good ones, good enough that they nearly eclipsed the bad ones of his own father. The fists and the bruises. The harsh words and the way they seemed to always cut him to the core. There were arguments at the Hutchins'. Loud voices and fights over toys and bickering and pushing each other's buttons.

But at the end of it, it was all coming from a place of love, and they always found their way back to it.

That's why Cora exploding had thrown them all for a loop.

Because they'd all—even part of Rafe had, too—had expected there to be a phone call apologizing for the outburst, telling them she had ordered some pizza and beer and that it was all good. To come back.

But she hadn't.

And now hours had passed.

And she still hadn't.

"It was all of us," Rome said. "We all know that she wasn't

happy with us barging in. We just didn't think that she would ever really get mad at us."

"She never has before." Jeremy sighed, studied his bottle. "Not really, anyway."

"Right," Wyatt said. "But this is different, and drinking all night isn't going to make it better."

"She's hurt and needs—"

"She's an adult," Rafe interjected, "and as much as it pains me to admit it. She can take care of herself."

"With bruised ribs and a sprained ankle?"

His fingers clenched on his beer. "Yes," he said, even though he hated the idea of her struggling on her own. "And she's adult enough to ask for help if she needs it. Plus," he added when it seemed like Asher was going to protest, "she has Kate and Heidi there."

Six sighs of relief.

No. Seven. Because he was relieved, too.

It wasn't going to be easy to step back and not jump into protective mode, but he knew they needed to figure out a way.

And that way couldn't be just drinking themselves into oblivion every night while watching *Die Hard* on repeat. Because it was Cora's favorite, and they were feeling sorry for themselves and—

The door to Wyatt's place slammed open.

They all jumped. Every last one of them. Beers jerking, splashing over the rim, dotting Wyatt's carpet. Then they were moving, jumping to their feet, and for Rafe's part, at least, that ascent was shaky.

So much beer.

But before he could summon his white knight to save Wyatt and the others from whoever had barged into his house, he realized who was there.

Who. Was. There.

A woman who looked very much like Cora.

But one who was infinitely scarier.

Cora's mom. Edy Hutchins. The woman who'd singlehandedly made his childhood bearable. And she was *scary*.

Scary *pissed*.

"What the fuck all have you been doing to my baby?"

It had taken them a long time to calm Edy down.

Mostly because she'd apparently come from Cora's place, where her beloved daughter had spent the day crying her eyes out.

Because of her brothers.

Which Edy grouped Rafe into.

He deserved it, but he also knew that he'd probably hurt Cora the most.

And that felt...like absolute shit.

"We're just looking after her," Jeremy said. "Like Dad made us promise."

Edy shot him a look. "Smothering your sister is not looking after her." Her eyes narrowed. "As you well know, since we've had this conversation before."

Jeremy sighed, but he didn't argue further, and none of them argued when she took over Wyatt's kitchen and whipped them all up some food that didn't come out of a box, bag, or can. Since this—and getting yelled at for the second time in one day by a woman who didn't make it a habit to yell—meant that the drinking had stopped, the sobering had commenced, it was finally safe enough for them to make their respective ways home.

With promises made to let Cora reach out first.

"You cool if I crash on your couch tonight?" he asked Wyatt. "I'll grab an Uber or something in the morning." And hope that Cora would let him in long enough to grab his stuff.

"Of course, man."

Edy was at the door, shrugging into her coat, but that exchange had her crossing over to him, poking him in the arm with her finger. "Oh no, buster, you're not getting out of it that easily. You're coming with me."

"I—" His eyes hit Wyatt's, who shrugged, seeming to say there was no sense in fighting it.

Which was exactly what Rafe had been thinking.

So, he nodded, grabbed his coat, and shoved his feet into his boots. "Okay, Mrs. Hutchins."

"Edy," she corrected, as she always did.

Rafe didn't bother arguing with that either, just nodded again and followed her out the front door to her car, a small red sedan she'd had from the moment Cora had left for college and she hadn't had to schlep kids around any longer.

He had to cram himself into the passenger's seat, his knees practically in his armpits.

Then they were on the road, zipping along the highway, making the forty-minute drive back to Cora's place.

"It's late," he said, eyes finally hitting on the time. "Are you going to be okay driving all the way to your house after dropping me off?"

Her gaze flicked to his. "You just can't help taking care of us, can you?"

And that was enough for him to make a study out of his hands. Oh look, he had a new scar across his knuckles. *How did that happen?*

"Me."

The blinker clicked as Edy changed lanes.

"Cora."

"All because your dad didn't take care of you."

He inhaled sharply. "I...he wasn't capable of giving me what I needed."

"Which is a very mature way to think about it, to spin it." She tapped her fingers on the steering wheel. "Unfortunately, it doesn't mean anything when you're still a scared, hurt little boy inside."

A sharp burst of pain.

"I'm—" Another breath, but he didn't know what to say to that, so he fell silent.

"You know, the first time Wyatt and Jeremy brought you home, I couldn't believe how tiny you were." She released a breath. "They were right around your age, but at least four inches taller and fifteen pounds heavier, and at six, that's a lot of inches and pounds." Her lips curved as she glanced at him. "But you've certainly filled out now, haven't you?"

"I'm not skinny and wearing youth extra small anymore, at least."

More curving before her eyes went back to the road. "Did you know that you were the first of the boys to hold Cora when we came home from the hospital?"

"I was?"

"Yup. You were."

He...thought he remembered holding her, but God, that was a long time ago.

"Quiet."

"What?"

"Always the quiet one," she said. "You were always so quiet and yet so protective over my kids. When you should have just been a baby, a little kid without any worries, you were always in your head, weighing every action, as though there were some scale in your mind and you thought that if you stepped out of line too much, did something we didn't like, and you'd tip it so that we didn't love you anymore."

His pulse picked up, palms going a little sweaty.

"But what you didn't understand, what I think you *still* don't understand, is that we love you. And love isn't something that is weighed out on a scale, one side filled with your good qualities, the other with your bad. Nothing will change that."

Another glance, just a bit of humor in her eyes. "Not even pushing my beloved daughter off a cliff."

He winced. "Asher is—"

"Going to beat himself up for an eternity, and then when he finally stops feeling guilty about it, will then be subjected to the torture of his brothers for another eternity?"

"That," he agreed.

She laughed. "Yup. I know my boys." Her eyes came to his again and she reached over, squeezed his hand. "And I love my boys. *All* my boys."

Fuck.

Now his eyes stung.

But she wasn't done.

"And I'll love them even if they don't make a choice I agree with, even if they make one my other boys don't agree with." She took the exit for Cora's place, halted at a signal at the end of the ramp and turned to him, gaze boring into his. "Because if they've made it with their heart and their mind, I *will* support them."

Sweat prickled on his nape. Did she know—?

"Because I trust my boys' hearts." The signal turned green. "And in case that wasn't clear, I consider you one of my boys, too, Rafe."

"Mrs.—"

"Edy," she corrected.

"I've always loved you all," he said, "you know that. I wouldn't do anything to jeopardize that."

Eyes so much like Cora's connected with his, but only for a moment before they were back on the road.

And that sweat continued to prickle.

"But honey, you know the others trust you, that if you made a decision"—eyes to his again, for just a second—"and if that decision was made with your heart and your mind...you know they'd come around, too."

What the fuck?

Did she know?

"I—"

But now her damned eyes stayed on the road, and when she began talking again, it wasn't about Cora or the boys. It was about arrangements for Jeremy and Wyatt's birthday dinner the following month—he was dating a woman and she wanted the scoop to see if it was going to last long enough to make it to a family dinner.

Spoiler alert: the woman was lovely and sweet (at least when they'd met up over drinks) and...she probably wouldn't because Wyatt was Wyatt.

And then they pulled into Cora's driveway.

"Is she going to hobble down the hall on her crutches and point a shotgun at me?"

Edy grinned, lifted her chin in the direction of the front door. "Only one way to find out." A laugh. "You feeling lucky?"

Twenty-Three

Cora

The knock at her door was tentative enough that she knew it belonged to one of the males of her family.

Whether that was a brother or a Rafe, she didn't know.

She *suspected* Rafe, since he was living at her house—not that she'd seen him since the blow-up on Monday—and not her brothers because her mom had apparently joined in on Cora's outburst and had given them *her* version of the riot act.

She'd gotten exactly one text from each of her brothers.

An apology and telling her they'd wait to hear from her.

All a variation on the same.

Which told her they'd gotten together and drafted up something together, and maybe that should have annoyed her, but she was already feeling more than a little guilty for yelling at the monsters—ungrateful much?—and yeah, she knew that she needed to continue to reinforce the boundaries and really, they couldn't just keep barging into her house and her bedroom.

And they needed to stop freaking out if she was dating someone.

But...she loved them.

So, she didn't want her life to not include them.

Rafe...well, unfortunately, she didn't want it to not include him either. She just needed...to figure out how to steel her heart so that it didn't hurt.

Brother and sister and that was it.

The knock came again, even more tentative this time.

But unlike before, the door didn't open, and no one popped their head in. Whoever was on the other side—and she should face it, it was Rafe, it had to be—just waited.

So, she called, "Come in."

The door opened slowly, and, yup, Rafe poked his head in. "Dinner's here," he said softly, holding up a bag of food.

Since she hadn't ordered anything, that was confusing, but because one of her siblings or friends probably had, she just shrugged and said, "Thanks."

Kate had left a tray for her, so she could eat in bed, and honestly, Cora was taking advantage of it. Her ribs still ached, and her ankle was feeling better, but she didn't think that she would be strutting around in heels any time soon.

Rafe grabbed the tray before she could, putting the food out on it, and pulling a can of soda from his pocket. "Need anything else?" he asked.

Yeah.

She needed him to get his head out of his ass.

But since he wasn't going to do that...

She just shook her head and thanked him again, but as he set the tray over her, their eyes locked, and her lungs...they froze.

"Cor," he whispered, leaning closer, his spicy scent filling her senses. "I'm sorry about before."

"I know."

His fingers stroked along her jaw, dipped down to trace along her throat. "I just—"

She covered his hand with her own. "Rafe. Just—"

His head dipped, mouth coming close enough that she felt his breath on her lips. Heat and need, desire and—

"No."

He blinked, straightened. "I'm—"

"God, please don't say you're sorry again."

"I wasn't going to."

Her brows lifted. "Bullshit."

He winced. "Okay, I might have been ready to apologize. It's just...you're Cora. I've loved you forever." Her heart began skipping around, tap-dancing along her rib cage. "Since you were a baby," he added quickly, and that sent the tap-dancing to a halt.

"Right."

"And I just don't like knowing I'm the one to hurt you. And I know your brothers feel the same way."

"I've already talked to Asher," she told him. "I put him out of his misery this morning."

"I know."

Of course, he did.

"And what, you thought he paved the way, so you would try for forgiveness, too?"

"Yeah," he muttered. "I just want us to all be okay." His expression told her that she was at least partially correct. Because there was something else in his eyes, in the line of his jaw that spoke to the inner conflict. Probably the same attraction and desire that had her skin prickling, her body so freaking aware of his, her breathing had elevated, her fingers tingled, her pussy ached.

"Right," she said. "Well, the good thing is that we are already okay. You made it clear what you want, and I'm not going to fight you on it." She forced a smile. "Brother and sister, right?"

He'd been lifting the tray up and over her, but her question had his hands shaking, the soda can tipping over. Thankfully, it hadn't been open. "Sorry." He set the tray down and righted it. "I...uh...thought we could eat and then I'll make some popcorn and hot chocolate and we can watch that new action movie with The Rock."

"As brother and sister," she repeated.

His fingers flexed. "Yup," he croaked. "Because I see you as my sister."

Cora rolled her eyes. "Right."

"So food, movie, and popcorn?"

"Don't you have anything better to do on a Friday than hang out with your sister?"

He chuckled. "Honestly? No."

That had her laughing, too, and good news, that actually hurt less than the day before. So...winning.

"What do you say?" he asked.

Besides that, he was a stupid man who was apparently determined to punish them both?

What *could* she say?

Either she could avoid him forever—difficult considering he was an integral part of her family and she'd have to deal with him any time she was around them, not to mention he was currently living in her freaking house—or...

She could accept what he was willing to give.

That one night.

And now, friendship.

"I say..." His shoulders went stiff, probably expecting her to tell him to fuck off. But she wasn't going to, she couldn't. "I say," she said again, "that movie night sounds good."

The relief on his face shouldn't have been so grand.

But it was.

And that made her feel...confused, weird, and...fuck this week had been a freaking whirlwind. She just wanted to feel normal, and movie night with popcorn and hot cocoa felt very normal (so did the longing for him, but then again, she'd had decades to get used to that, so that was new?).

He settled the tray over her, disappeared a few minutes later, and reappeared with a plate for himself.

Then he sat at the end of the bed as they ate, and eventually they paused the movie for hot cocoa and popcorn preparations, for him, and bathroom needs, for her.

It wasn't until buildings were exploding that he relaxed and didn't go stiff every single time their hands brushed in the popcorn bowl. It wasn't until the end credits rolled and he gathered everything up, that it felt like the old days, like they were sitting on a couch in the basement of her mom's old house, and she was going to doze off before he carried her up to bed.

But instead, Rafe was already *in* her bed.

"Right," he said, his hands full of cups and bowls and trash, "I'll just let you get some rest."

"Yeah." She studied his eyes, wondering if this was all it would ever be.

Knowing it was.

"Night," she whispered.

With a nod, he slipped out the door, mugs rattling as he closed it behind him, and she was left with the sounds of the credits playing, trying to figure out if she felt sad or resolved or numb...or all three.

Then she saw the bag leftover from dinner, sitting on the floor next to her nightstand.

Then she saw the name on the receipt tacked to the *outside* of that bag.

Rafe.

He'd ordered her dinner.

He'd orchestrated the whole thing.

And...then she was as confused as ever.

And...then she woke up, and Rafe was gone.

And yup.

Confused.

She should buy stock in it.

She cursed as she began to drag the coffee table across the room, ribs screaming and stitches pulling.

And itching.

"You know, honey..."

Cora froze, whipped around—fucking stupid, she knew—and bit back a wince as she faced her mother, leaning against the wall, arms crossed, and watching the scene.

It had been a week since her injury.

A week since Rafe had disappeared in the night and not come back.

But who was counting?

Not her.

Nope.

No way.

She shook that off, internally, not physically, because she was not about that rib pain. "Hi, Mom. I didn't know you were coming. Do you want something to eat? Or some coffee?"

Her mom's lips twitched, probably because she had instilled all those good host merits into Cora.

"No, honey," she said, then straightened, inclined her head to the kitchen, "but I *did* bring you lunch."

She held up a Molly's bag, and Cora could have kissed her.

Hell, she was Cor's mom, so she *could* kiss her.

So, she did, limping over and pressing one to her cheek. "Thank you."

Her mom smiled, wrapped her arm around Cora's waist and led her into the kitchen. "You're my baby," she said by way of explanation as they pulled out stools and started to sit. "You *know*," her mom began again once her ass hit the chair, and Cora braced. "You don't have to do it *all* on your own."

Cora gritted her teeth, knew exactly who'd told on her. "Kate."

A shrug. "Kate did call me after you sent them all away yesterday, but that's not what I meant, honey."

"They did enough," she said. "They have lives and partners, and Kate is like nine million months pregnant. Plus, Kelsey bent over backward to get me a job back at Robotech—"

"And by *bent over backward*, you mean she had one conversation with Abby...who's her friend and clearly wanted you back with the company." Her mom lifted a brow. "Because *you're good at your job.*"

"I—" She sighed. "She *got* me a job, Mom. I was unhappy, and she pulled some strings to get me a job like she was ordering a Happy Meal in the drive-through—"

"*She* reconnected you with someone who was sad to see you leave the company and very happy to bring you back on to do a job you're very qualified for?"

"*Mom.*"

A tap to the tip of her nose. "What I'm saying is that you don't always have to do everything on your own."

"I know."

Her mom unrolled the top of the bag, began pulling out containers, setting them on the island. "You *know*, except for the fact that you push everyone away who tries to do something for you."

"Mom—"

"Especially Asher, baby, you know that he's feeling guilty. You know that he would feel better if he could help you out a little bit—"

"It wasn't a big deal. You know it was an accident, and that I'll be fine—"

"Yes, honey. You know. *I* know that, but Asher is going to

eat himself alive for a while yet." She let out a long, slow breath and squeezed Cora's hand. "Baby, what you need to understand is that sometimes being so strong and on your own and isolated and tough and taking no prisoners can hurt you." Another squeeze. "And sometimes it can hurt more than yourself."

She inhaled.

"Because, baby, sometimes it hurts the people who we love, too."

Cora stared down at the salad in front of her, the small cup of soup, and saw the care in this small gesture. The *love* in it. And...a curl of guilt sliced through her. Because—fuck—what kid liked to know that the nonsense their mom was spouting was right?

And she *was* right.

That curl of guilt tightened.

"I see you're getting me."

Because ugh. Yeah, she was.

Which was why she reached into her pocket, tugged out her cell, and made a call.

He answered on the first ring.

"Ash? Do you think you can come over? I could use a little help."

Twenty-Four

Rafe

He was exhausted, covered in sawdust, and had spent the last month busting ass in L.A.

Now he was back in the Bay Area, had spent the day at the warehouse, and finally, *finally* he was going to go to his new apartment.

It was small, and mostly empty, the stuff he'd shipped up from SoCal not having arrived yet.

Tonight was the air mattress night.

Tomorrow his belongings would arrive.

And tomorrow night...he would see Cora again.

It was Jeremy and Wyatt's birthday—he'd already wrapped the signed puck from his favorite Gold player, Brit Plantain, and left it in Edy's care—but they were all getting together tomorrow night for meatloaf, potatoes, and Edy's homemade red velvet cheesecake.

Family tradition said it was the birthday boy—or girl's choice—of meal and Edy-prepared dessert.

Then they'd play board games until curse words were exchanged.

Which happened sooner or later, depending on which games were chosen.

UNO? Within five minutes (which meant that it was just a night of curse words that Mrs. Hutchins pretended not to hear).

Ticket to Ride? They might make it ten before the cursing commenced (also ignored by Edy).

Munchkin? Basically, from the beginning.

So, really, it was a lot of cursing, a lot of games, a lot of competitive spirit...and a lot of Edy ignoring the misbehavior of her grown children.

But it was fun, and he wouldn't miss a Hutchins Birthday Get Together.

Even if he knew it was going to churn up everything with Cora all over again.

Even if there was nothing to churn up because it was already in the front of his mind. Because it hadn't gone anywhere.

Because he'd spent nearly every waking moment working his ass off, trying to *not* think about Cora.

And failing anyway.

He'd had more wet dreams...

"Packing up?"

He nearly impaled himself with his hammer—and not the one that was misbehaving and waking him up with soiled boxers like a goddamned teenager.

Clearing his throat, he turned to face Teresa.

Who looked like she was fighting a smile.

He glared.

She stopped fighting it and *just* smiled. "You know how I gave you advice that you told me was correct a while ago. About Cora," she added, like he hadn't known exactly what she meant.

"Uh-huh," he muttered, shoving his hammer into his toolbox.

"Well, I also have some advice about a stubborn man with the woman he's in love with."

His heart clenched, but he didn't say anything, just snapped the latches on his toolbox and started for the door.

"See you later!" Teresa called. "You know, unless you get your head out of your ass and run away with Cora!"

He stopped, turned around. "You know what?"

She sauntered over, punched him lightly in the shoulder. "What?"

"You're fired."

Laughter in the air, her arm lacing with his as she led them both out the door. "You know you would never fire me. You love me"—a grin up at him—"just not in the same way that you love *Cora*." She extended the -ora in Cora for a good five seconds.

"I swear to God, T—"

A beatific smile. "Also, Mrs. H invited me tomorrow, and you know I'm not going to miss one of her dinners—"

"Or the chance to torment Jeremy by beating him at Monopoly."

Teresa laughed. "That, too. But you know that I've seen you two together, and you know that I was right about the other stuff"—she wagged her brows—"just like I'm usually right about *everything*."

He sighed. "Teresa."

She blinked up at him innocently. "What?"

"I swear, sometimes I wonder why we're friends."

"No," she said. "You sometimes wonder how empty your life was without me, and then you get on your knees and thank the Goddess that—"

He covered her mouth with his palm.

And...she licked him.

"Ugh! Gross!" he exclaimed, wiping his wet palm on his thigh. "You're disgusting."

"And you love me." She pursed her lips, blew him a kiss. "You know it."

He did. Spit and all. "Shut up, T."

She smirked, hit the code for the alarm, and he locked up, right as she glanced up at him, still smiling beatifically. "Also, can I have a ride to Mrs. H's tomorrow?"

He sighed.

But because Teresa was Teresa and he was him, all he did was shake his head.

And she knew that was a yes.

Because he cared for the people in his life and took care of them...

Even if that meant part of him didn't get the same care.

More exhaustion, this time paired with a sense of satisfaction.

No air mattress tonight.

His whole bedroom was set up, as was his kitchen and family room. He still had a closet full of stuffed duffles and suitcases instead of clothes that were hung up or put away, but the toughest areas were moved in.

Tomorrow, he'd deal with the clothes.

Tonight, he was girding his loins.

Cora would be there, and he had to forget about their night. Had to go back to her just being Cora, his little sister and—

Bullshit.

They *couldn't* go back.

So, his new strategy was ignoring that night, the attraction, and pretending that everything was great!

Yup.

With an exclamation point.

Because it all *was* great. He had a place to stay. His business was on to bigger and better things. He had friends and the family he'd built.

So, it was all perfect.

Or as perfect as he could ever hope for, especially with his doorbell going. And the knock. And the woman standing on the other side of his door.

"I'm ready for my Uber, baby!" Teresa called.

He sighed. "You're riding in the front seat."

"And then," Teresa said, scooping up a truly huge bite of red velvet cake and shoving it into her mouth, somehow speaking clearly despite the mass of frosting and baked good, "just because I'm me, I made him chauffeur me all the way out here."

Rafe rolled his eyes.

Cora giggled.

And all six brothers looked relieved. Because Cor was laughing and hadn't kicked them out or yelled at them again. Probably because Wyatt's girlfriend, Tiffany, was there, so she was on her best behavior, but also maybe because she'd forgiven them.

At least forgiven her brothers.

She wasn't giving him the cold shoulder exactly. But...she was distant.

And he didn't like it.

Which was fucking stupid because, of course, she was distant. He'd erected that space between them when she wanted more.

It was just...

He didn't like it.

Fucking moron.

Quietly, he got up from the table, slipped from the room. Teresa was in full story-telling mode, so they wouldn't notice if he took a few minutes to himself. The back deck had twinkly lights crisscrossed overhead that he'd installed a few years back, and he'd put in a sunken fire pit that Edy had found a picture of on Pinterest just a few months before.

Weekend projects for his mom.

Because his own was dead and gone.

Because he'd never even known his mother, and his father becoming a single parent without warning hadn't gone over well. Rafe's dad had died a couple of years back, and maybe it made him a bad person, but Rafe hadn't cared. Hell, he would have been happy for the miserable asshole to depart the earth a few years before that.

He'd had no problem making it known that Rafe was a burden.

But then again, he'd had no problem taking Rafe's money or becoming Rafe's burden. Because as much as he'd wanted to treat his dad the same way he'd been treated, Rafe hadn't been able to.

He'd paid for his in-home nurse. Hell, Rafe had paid for *all* of it—electricity, mortgage, cable, internet, new clothes, fucking *diapers,* and bedpans.

And never once had he been made to feel like a son.

Just a burden.

Just a cash cow.

"Hell," he muttered, walking by the fire pit that was blazing and moving to the railing, leaning his elbows on it. "Fucking hell."

"I know what's the matter."

His head jerked, and he saw that Jeremy was in the shadows. "Avoiding Teresa?"

One half of Jeremy's mouth turned up. "Of course, I am. That woman—" He sighed and shook his head.

Rafe let that go.

He didn't need some next-level Teresa ESP skills to know

that Jeremy was into her (even though Teresa's skills seemed to exclude her interactions with Jeremy and how much he was into her, and...see? She did have limitations...and they included her being closed to any sort of relationship that involved her heart).

"But that's not who I'm talking about."

A thread of cold down his spine.

He'd caught himself watching Cora far too much that night. Had needed to force his gaze away from hers many times over the evening.

Too many times.

Jeremy ambled over, leaned on the railing. "I know, Rafe," he said. "It's all good. We don't have to talk about it, but I know that it's a rough time with the anniversaries."

He glanced out over the darkened back yard, struggling for a moment to come up with what anniversaries Jer was talking about. Then he got it...and maybe he should feel like shit because he'd just been thinking about the old bastard kicking the bucket. But he hadn't thought about his mom too much.

Not ever.

She was dead because of him.

Okay, so he was old enough and mature enough to understand it wasn't exactly because of him. His mother had suffered from postpartum depression and had committed suicide.

Because she hadn't gotten help.

Because people didn't really talk about it, or his dad hadn't helped her get the help she needed, or her doctors hadn't seen—

She was gone.

It was Rafe's fault.

Those had been the words from his father. Those had been the words that defined his childhood. Those had been the words that had defined *him*.

Until Mr. And Mrs. Hutchins had changed his mind.

He wasn't a burden. He was a gift.

But...he didn't know if that was something he would ever

truly believe. Because otherwise, he would just go for it with Cora, wouldn't he? He wouldn't be such a coward, too worried to gain the disapproval of her brothers.

Because Edy...she knew.

She'd caught his eye enough times that night, and paired with the conversation in the car, he knew she knew, and he knew that she would support him.

It was just Jeremy and Wyatt, Eli and Asher, Rome and Rowan.

How could he risk them?

But he was starting to think...how could he not?

How could he sit with Cora, eat and drink, talk and laugh with her and know what they had and know what they *could* have...and know he was taking that away from them?

Because he was scared to try.

"Fuck," he muttered, rubbing a hand over his forehead.

What a fucking mess, and it all seemed to be moving toward this inevitable conclusion. Like what was going to happen when he couldn't resist her any longer, when he couldn't resist.

This was all just going to blow up and—

Jeremy bumped him on the arm. "I'm sorry, man."

"I'm okay," he said. "It's not my parents. That's just...reality. I mean, I never knew my mom, and my dad was my dad." He blew out a breath. "Truthfully, if I'm being honest"—he glanced up at Jer—"the anniversary of your dad dying is a hell of a lot harder on me."

Jeremy was quiet for a long time. "I'm sorry your dad was such a dick."

"I'm sorry your dad wasn't and that my asshole of a sperm donor got to live a long life and your dad didn't."

"He was as much your dad as he was all of ours, you know that, right?" Jer cleared his throat, gaze on the yard. "My dad...I don't know how he did it, but he never made us feel like we were missing out, not even when there were more of us."

Rafe watched the trees rustle in the distance, the cool evening breeze starting to pick up. "I don't know how I was lucky enough to become one of you."

Jeremy went stiff then punched Rafe hard in the arm. "What the fuck, man?"

"Ow." Rafe rubbed the spot. "What the fuck to *you?*"

"*Lucky to become one of us?*" Jer shook his head. "You know that we love you, right? You know that we're the ones who feel lucky to have *you*, yeah?"

"I—" Rafe sighed. "Look. I know what I bring to the table, and I know what you guys bring—*ow!*"

Another punch. This time harder.

"Dude, what the fuck is going on with your head?"

"I'm fine. I just—"

The door slid open behind them. Asher and Eli sauntered out, took one look at him and Jer and lifted their brows. "What's going on?"

Jer shoved Rafe lightly. "This one is being a dumbass."

Asher grinned. "What else is new?"

"Let it go, Jer," he muttered. "Let's have our heart-to-heart another time."

Jeremy bent close, studied him closely with narrowed eyes. "I'll let it go. For tonight only. Because next time I see you being a dumbass, we're having the heart-to-heart, even *if* I have to tie you down and force you to listen to me."

He forced a grin. "Kinky."

"Idiot." Another punch. "Come on, let's go have another beer and enjoy our time before Teresa destroys us all in *Ticket to Ride*.

Twenty-Five

Cora

Her shoulder was aching, absolutely aching, but then again, she'd been pulling some long hours at her computer over the last month.

Partly, because she felt obligated to complete the promised projects for Dale, even though it had taken her longer than her final two weeks, since she'd been laid up for most of them. Partly because she'd hit the ground running at RoboTech, helping them kick off the marketing plan for their newest children's robot.

The Hunter Five was wicked cool.

It could be taken apart and put back together. It could be coded to complete simple tasks.

And for every robot sold, RoboTech donated one to schools.

Epic, right?

She thought so. And she especially thought it was epic to have a boss that respected work hours. No emails expected to be replied to in the middle of the night, no six A.M. starts in the office. No staying late or working through lunch.

After spending almost a year without that, Cora had almost forgotten what it was like to have a normal life.

Especially, the last couple of weeks.

And now...family dinner time and Rafe pretending that nothing had happened and...yeah, it sucked, but that was the way it was going to be, so there was no point in flogging that dead horse.

"Are you all right, honey?" her mom asked.

Cora frowned, coming out of her own head (it was easy to get lost in it when she was drying the various pots and pans that her mom had used to cook dinner, not to mention the special cake plates and forks that were absolutely not allowed to go into the dishwasher), and realized she was rubbing her shoulder again, the towel dragging across the exposed skin of her throat.

"Cor?" her mom asked again, putting down her own towel, brows drawing together.

She shook herself. "Honestly, I'm just a little fuzzy headed. This last month has been a lot, and my body isn't fully recovered."

"Your ribs?"

Cora nodded. "Yeah, they're tender, and then my ankle still feels a bit weak." She shook her head when her mom got that worried Mom Look and put her hand up before her mom could really get going. "I'm not pushing it too hard, Mom. I promise. Dale's in the rearview, and you know the climate at RoboTech is a lot better. The hours and workload are reasonable. It's just... going to take some time for me to recharge."

Her mom came close, leaning back against the counter next to her and wrapping an arm around Cora's shoulders.

Which hurt.

She bit back a hiss.

"Baby," her mom began.

She shifted, rolled her shoulder. "It's fine, Mom. I promise. Just too much time on my laptop and my brother pushing me off a cliff." Her mom rolled her eyes and sighed. "Plus, my period is about to start. I'm so crampy. Actually," she said. "I'm going to get some ibuprofen from your bathroom, then I'll come back and finish these up."

Her mom kissed her on the cheek. "I'll finish up here and then get the heating pad."

"You're a goddess."

A grin. "If only you'd known that when you were a teenager."

Cora chuckled...then winced.

Her mom nudged her toward the stairs. "You just get your pills, and maybe a pad, you know"—her mom made a face—"just in case nature decides to bless you."

"Ew," Cora said.

A shrug. "Well, you're the one who wore white pants."

There was that.

"Anyway," her mom pushed off the counter. "Pills, pad, and then go out and get the boys. I think Teresa is getting restless." A nod toward the family room where Teresa was setting up *Ticket to Ride* (Wyatt's choice) with Tiffany helping her, and considering that Teresa was practically vibrating out of her skin, her competitive nature well-known and already showing.

"Right," she murmured. "I'm on all of it."

"Good." A kiss to the top of her head.

Cora draped her towel over the edge of the sink and hit the hall, climbing the stairs, and hating how weak she felt.

Ribs. Shoulder. Ankle.

She needed to heal because it really shouldn't be this difficult to climb one flight of stairs. Hell, she was puffing like she'd run a fucking marathon by the time she reached the top, and the shoulder pain eclipsed everything else.

Well, everything else except for her cramps.

Her mom was right. She'd better get a pad, too. Last thing

she wanted to do was ruin these pants. They'd cost over a hundred dollars and were dry clean only.

Rolling her eyes at her idiocy—because she was an idiot who'd spent over a hundred dollars on white pants when she spilled on herself at regular intervals—she huffed her way into the *en suite* attached to her mom's bedroom and helped herself to the medicine cabinet.

Pad. Check.

Ibuprofen. Check.

Water from the tap to take said ibuprofen. Check.

Head still slightly muzzy and cramps increasing in intensity? Check.

Perfect.

Sighing, she left the bathroom and made her way down the stairs, along the hallway, and out the slider onto the back deck.

The boys were gathered around the fire pit, deep in discussion, and they didn't hear her.

And what *she* heard had her feet freezing, retreating, taking her back into the shadows.

"Admit it," Asher was saying, "you like Teresa, and you don't really care when she beats you."

Okay that wasn't the part that drew her back into the shadows. In fact, hearing that, she grinned, started forward, mouth open and ready to join in on the teasing.

That was one thing about growing up with six brothers.

She had gotten damned good at dishing out teasing.

And the not-so-secret secret that Jeremy liked Teresa was the perfect topic for that teasing.

"Fuck off," Jeremy muttered, swigging out of his bottle. "What's more important is that one"—he nodded at Rafe—"being an idiot."

"*You* fuck off," Rafe muttered.

See? She needed to be in the shadows for this. Because if what he was being stupid about was *her*, then she shouldn't be hearing this, shouldn't be part of this conversation. She should turn around and come back in five or come back dragging her feet loudly so they'd hear her.

But all she did was stand in the shadows and idly rub her aching shoulder, hoping the pain killers kicked in soon.

"He thinks he's lucky to have us."

Rome snorted. "And let me guess, he doesn't get that we're lucky to have him, too."

She inhaled sharply.

Lucky for *her,* the boys were too busy yelling at Rafe to hear her.

"Seriously, man?" Eli said.

"What the fuck?" Wyatt.

"Dumbass." Asher.

Only Rowan was silent, studying Rafe in the quiet way he had. "You know, Rome and I don't have a ton of memories of our dad, because we were the youngest besides Cora when he died."

"She has it the worst, but...it was hard," Rome said. "Especially those of us who had less time with him."

Cora bit her lip.

"But we remember enough," Rowan added in that twin way of theirs, smoothly finishing each other's thoughts. "We know he taught us that when you love someone, *you're* the lucky one."

Great. Now her eyes burned.

Because her brothers had told her that so many times over the years, and to know they meant it, that'd they'd get all gushy without reservation to make sure Rafe knew they meant it...

Yeah, tears were imminent.

Things might not have worked out between them, but he deserved to know that he was loved.

Especially since his dad had been so abusive, had messed him up deep inside, had him questioning the love, thinking that he wasn't good enough for it, that he could lose it if he stepped out of line.

And that was the crux of the problem between them, wasn't it?

She'd always known that her brothers would love her.

No matter what.

And Rafe's foundation of love was based on a mother who'd committed suicide (left him) and a father who'd been abusive (emotionally with plenty of gaslighting thrown in).

Her stomach clenched. Hard.

Because she realized she'd pushed him in the wrong way.

She'd asked him to choose because she'd known that her brothers would always love her, would love him. That they might be pissed and grumpy and maybe a punch or two would be thrown, but she knew they would come around.

Because Rafe had a big heart, and the love he gave to them all was beautiful.

Because they loved him in the same way.

But it wasn't fair for her to push him to give something when his past was...bad. That was the simplest word for it, and also the most basic because that kind of trauma didn't just go away, even being folded in the Hutchins' clan couldn't cure it.

"You wouldn't think that if you knew."

Silence.

At least, she thought her brothers had fallen silent because it was hard to hear anything, not with her pulse pounding in her ears. Her breathing seemed loud, too, not that anyone else seemed to hear it.

Then Jer spoke. "What do you mean?"

Rafe rubbed a hand over his face, and she knew, *knew,* he was going to sabotage this, try to prove to himself that see? He'd never deserved it. The love wasn't stable. It was something that could be ripped away, used to punish.

Just like his dad had done.

God, she was an idiot.

She'd thought that because he'd been one of them for so long that he would know their love for him wouldn't go away.

But clearly, he didn't.

Because he'd reached some dead end in his mind, and he was ready to just...implode it all. To end it. To impale himself on his sword and destroy everything he'd held so tight.

He sighed. "I didn't mean for it to happen. I want you to know that."

Wyatt frowned. Rowen looked retrospect. The rest of her brothers were in various stages of confusion.

And she was standing in the shadows, stomach cramping, hyperventilating, and feeling dizzy.

"What are you talking about?"

Rafe's gaze went to Wyatt's. "Shit, man. It's your birthday. I shouldn't—"

"Dude, I don't give a fuck about my birthday. I want to know what's put that fucking look on your face."

"I slept—"

She couldn't let him do this.

Heart pounding, she lurched out of the shadows, pain ricocheting up her side. "It's time to play *Ticket to—*"

Seven gazes whipping her direction.

"Cora?" Rafe said. "Are you—?"

His gorgeous face went unfocused.

He moved toward her. She took another step, so terrified he was doing this that she was shaky and out of breath.

"Don't—"

Her legs gave out.

Twenty-Six

Rafe

"L*ook, I slept with her, okay? I had sex with Cora, and I'm fucking in love with her and—"*

Those were the words flying through his mind.

But he didn't see Cora coming, didn't expect to see her lurching out of the shadows, her expression odd, her skin a sick, sallow color.

What the fuck?

"Cora?" he said, moving toward her. "Are you—?"

She clutched her side. "Don't—"

She collapsed.

Cursing, he moved toward her, trying to grab her before she hit the ground. Her legs had crumpled beneath her body, splayed at strange angles, and her lower half...

His gut seized.

Because her lower half was stained with blood.

He'd pushed his way into the back of the ambulance.

Anyone else probably would have been a better choice, a saner choice.

But Cora had collapsed.

She was bleeding.

A lot.

A first, Edy had thought it was just her period, laughing off their shouts. But then when she realized Cora was unconscious, saw the amount of blood soaking her clothes, she'd yelled for someone to call 9-1-1.

Everyone had moved.

Jeremy had already been making the call before Edy had freaked, and the rest of them buzzed around, grabbing towels, clearing some space, doing...stuff—

He'd lost track.

Because he was holding onto Cora's hand, talking to her, telling her everything that had been going through his head from the moment he'd decided to just tell her brothers and fuck it all, because he couldn't keep the secret any longer, couldn't keep pretending—

Not with Cora.

She deserved better.

She deserved to be more than a secret.

She deserved for him to choose her, above all else.

But he hadn't gotten to tell her that. Not while she was conscious, and he had no way of knowing if she could hear him.

He did know her brothers had heard him. That Teresa and Edy had as well.

So, the cat was out of the bag.

And he didn't give a fuck.

Because...her hand had been limp when they'd rushed her through the double doors of the emergency department, sliding from his so easily.

She could be gone, just that easily.

He might not—

A sob bubbled up in his throat, but he choked it down, dug his fists into his eyes. He'd wasted—

A hand on his shoulder had him looking up.

Jeremy was crouched in front of him, and the look that was in his eyes told Rafe everything. "Breathe."

Movement at his side, Wyatt sitting next to him then at his other, Edy taking the other seat and weaving their hands together. "Has the doctor come out?"

He shook his head. "No."

She squeezed his hand. "So, then we wait."

So...that was what they did.

For hours.

And still, they heard not one word from the doctors and nurses in the back.

"Cora Hutchins?"

His eyes had slid closed, but the sound of Cora's name had him lurching to his feet, along with the rest of her family.

The young doctor who had called, saw the movement, and wove her way toward their huddle. "Cora Hutchins?" she asked again.

He nodded.

"That's my daughter," Edy said, clenching his hand.

"Cora is out of surgery."

He inhaled sharply. They hadn't even known she was *in* surgery. It had all moved so fast in the ambulance with them getting an IV in, rushing down the roads to the hospital, taking her through the doors.

"Do you know what an ectopic pregnancy is?"

Rafe frowned, shook his head, but Edy's breath in was sharp, and she nodded. "Oh no," she whispered.

"From what we could see, she was about six weeks along. But the good news is that she's stable for now," the petite brunette said, "but she lost a lot of blood and one of her fallopian tubes burst—that was the source of the bleeding. Unfortunately, we had to remove it, but her other tube is intact, and she shouldn't have any issues getting pregnant again, though they'll want to watch her closely when she is ready to get pregnant again."

Pregnant.

Pregnant.

"Can we see her?" Edy asked, and thank fuck for that, because he was spiraling and doing the math and realizing that he'd nearly killed her.

He'd nearly killed her.

He'd hurt her and *nearly killed her.*

"All family here?"

His head shot up.

He opened his mouth to say he was just a friend, but Edy just clamped down on his fingers and said, "Yes."

The doctor nodded. "They'll be transferring her from a recovery room to a normal bed, and once she's settled, two of you at a time can see her. I'll send someone out with the room number and visiting hour information soon, okay?"

"Okay," he whispered.

"Now," she said, "the events will have been quite traumatic, and she may need some counseling. I'll make sure the social worker rounds on her, but I want you to keep that in mind and to be open to some for yourselves as well."

He nodded, not knowing what the rest of the group was doing because he was hearing the doctor, but he was also spiraling and in his own head, and all he could think was because he'd slept with her, because he hadn't used a condom, because—

A rough hand on his arm, dragging him from the waiting room of the emergency department, through the automatic doors, and out into the cold evening air.

All the air was squeezed out of him when he was shoved against a wall, his back colliding hard with the brick of the building. Pain shot up and down his back, along his skull, his legs, and then the fist was coming for him.

He watched it get closer.

Braced for impact.

Readied for the pain to increase. Hell, he was *dying* for that pain, desperate to feel it.

Anything so that he wouldn't be feeling *this*.

Guilt.

And like he'd truly fucked up the best thing he'd ever had.

But that fist didn't collide with his face as he'd expected. Or not hard, anyway. Instead, it tapped against his nose lightly. "*That's* for fucking my sister and knocking her up. This—" A breath. "*This* is for loving her like she deserves."

Rafe's eyes shot open.

Too late.

But it wasn't another punch—a real one. This time, Jeremy yanked him into a hug, clamping his hand onto the back of Rafe's neck and holding him tight.

And fuck if his eyes didn't tear up.

"Dude," Jeremy said, releasing him from the hug, though he kept his hand on the back of Rafe's neck. "If it was anyone else, *anyone*—"

Rafe swallowed, eyes shutting tight.

"But you and her make sense. And..."

He opened his eyes again, saw Wyatt had stepped close. "We knew."

"What?"

"We've known you love her for years," Jeremy said, leaning on the wall next to him. "It just took you long enough to realize it."

"I—" He frowned. "*What?*"

Wyatt rolled his eyes. "Dude, the way you jumped to stay at

her place? How you were always the first one to run the assholes off? The guilt on your face whenever you looked at her the last weeks?"

"But you got all in my face in the bedroom—"

"Yeah," Wyatt said, "because she's my *sister*. I'm going to get in the face of anyone who wants to get into her pants, even if that man is my brother."

Asher shuddered. "Fuck, man, don't say it like that."

Eli smirked. "How else is he supposed to say it? It's like some fetish film—"

Rowan clamped a hand over his mouth then shoved his bigger, older brother away, pushing by him and coming up to Rafe. "She's going to be okay. *You're* going to be okay. We're all going to be—"

"Let me guess," Eli muttered. "Okay?"

Rome punched him.

"The point is, we know that you'll love her the way she deserves."

"Yeah," Asher said, "and if you hurt her, we'll just push you off a cliff."

That got smirks, all except for Rafe, who had just been dropping into an alternate fucking universe. "I—" He shoved a hand through his hair. "I don't understand what's happening right now."

Jeremy squeezed his shoulder. "What's happening is that you treat our sister right, it'll all be good, whether you two work out forever, or not. As long as you love her and treat her right, then the rest we'll figure out."

"Like not punching you in the balls because you want to fuck our sis—"

"Jesus," Rowan muttered. "Treat her right, and we're good, yeah?"

Rafe blinked. "I...um...I...yeah. I want to give her the world."

Another squeeze from Jeremy. "That's all we want for her, too."

"So just breathe, and let's all be there for her, okay?"

He still felt like he'd been dropped into an alternate universe, but Cora was inside in a hospital bed and her brothers weren't killing him, so that's all he knew for the moment.

Fuck. No. He knew more than that. Because he knew that he needed Cora to know how much he loved her and, fuck, he needed to find a way to make up for leaving her, for just walking out and not contacting her, for pretending their night together, their time at her house, the years they'd spent building their friendship, their love (even though it hadn't been romantic until recently) hadn't been enough.

He needed to make up for making her feel like she wasn't enough—

Fuck.

He needed to grovel.

And he needed to do it big.

Twenty-Seven

Cora

There was a weight at her side.

And heavy ones on her eyelids, making it nearly impossible to open her eyes.

Had she fallen?

Had she...ouch, it felt like she'd been run over by a Mack truck...had she been pushed off another cliff?

Except...it was quiet.

And if she'd fallen at her mom's house, it wouldn't be quiet. They'd be fussing all over her and—

There was the sound of a door scraping open, and her brows drew together, mostly because the scraping was followed by... someone touching her.

What the fuck?

Her eyes flew open.

"Oh, hey there." The nurse at her side had frozen. Then she carefully smoothed the blanket she'd been lifting. "Do you remember where you are?"

Cora shook her head.

"You're in the hospital, Cora."

She frowned, trying to remember. She'd been so dizzy at her mom's house. "Did I fall?"

A nod. "Yeah, honey. You fell and were transported by ambulance. You've been in the hospital for a little over twenty-four hours."

"I—" What the hell?

The nurse patted her hand. "Let me get the doctor, sweetie. She'll be able to answer your questions."

"I...okay."

The door opened and closed again, and then the nurse was gone, but she hardly noticed because she'd finally focused on the heavy weight at her side.

Rafe.

Of course he was there, dark circles beneath his eyes, stubble on his cheeks.

And waking up, as though some part of him had realized she was finally awake.

"Cor?" he asked, lacing his fingers through hers as he sat up. "Oh, my God," he whispered. "You're awake. Are you okay? How are you feeling—?"

The door slid open, and a short brunette walked in, a stethoscope hanging around her neck. "Hi, I'm Dr. Philips."

And then, after greetings were exchanged, Cora felt the world shift beneath her feet.

She'd been pregnant?

But she wasn't now and...how could she be grieving for a baby she hadn't even known she'd had?

The world closed in on her, reduced down to the doctor and her words, the pain in her side, and the strength of Rafe's fingers around hers.

And then the doctor was gone.

And then she was crying.

And...

Everything was the same, and yet everything was different, and...it was all wrong.

She'd fallen asleep again.

There was a weight all along her side, one that had her opening eyes, much more aware this time around.

A baby.

Part of her was grieving for a baby she hadn't even known existed...

God.

Why was she doing that? She hadn't even known, didn't even *want* to be pregnant, and—

And her mental asshole just needed to chill the fuck out.

Because it was part of Rafe and her, and she was allowed to grieve and—

She stopped.

Nearly bolted upright in the bed.

Because it was part of her and Rafe. Because *her and Rafe*. Because...

"Oh, my God," she whispered, eyes flying open, and she didn't quite bolt upright, but she did slowly push herself into a seated position, which then jostled that weight slumped behind her on the bed on her uninjured side.

Which jostled *Rafe*.

Because Rafe was there.

Next to her. *In bed* next to her, his arm carefully tucked around her shoulders.

Fuck.

Rafe was there, and suddenly everything she'd been hearing and thinking and realizing and panicking over before she collapsed slammed right into the forefront of her mind.

Rafe. Her brothers. They couldn't find out. She knew it would all be fine, but Rafe didn't, and if he thought he would lose—

"Rafe," she hissed, shaking him. "*Rafe!*"

He bolted upright, nearly clocking her in the face with an errant hand, controlled just in time. His dark circles, which she'd made a brief study of before her world had come crashing down, were even darker, even deeper, heavy grooves inching up the sides of his mouth, curving outward along the corners of his eyes.

Exhausted.

He looked so exhausted, she nearly had him lie back down and go back to sleep, fuck her brothers and their inane urge to protect her from men.

She'd tell them and—

Voices in the hall.

Voices she recognized because they belonged to the big protective lugs that were her brothers.

Voices that were going to murder, death, kill Rafe if they found him in bed with her.

"Rafe," she hissed again. "You've got to get up, to get out of this bed."

His arm tightened slightly, but then to her great relief—or maybe disappointment, because she'd had this man's name in her diary so many times over the years, so having him hold her like this was...magical.

Magic—

Fuck.

She needed to get her brain working.

"Rafe!"

He blinked and slowly moved his arm, shifting it out from behind her and climbing out before gently helping her lie back down onto the mattress.

"What the hell do you think you were doing?" she asked, as the door began to open.

Then halted, voices gathering out in the hall.

He'd been turning away, settling into a chair at the side of the bed, but her question had him freezing, spinning back toward her, and cupping her cheek in his palm, leaning close, enveloping her in his spicy scent all over again.

"Cor—"

Her pulse raced. Her heart got a little fluttery.

And then...

The door opened a little farther.

She jerked away, slamming her head into the—thankfully—soft bed, the pillow that had been thoughtfully fluffed. "Rafe, you can't—" A sharp shake of her head. "They— I know that you can't lose them—"

His face changed, emotions scrolling rapid fire across his face.

Too fast for her to process.

But before she could press him, ask him to slow down and explain the flurry in his expression, the door swung wide, and her family rolled in.

All of them.

Descended.

Hugs and crowding around her bed, and it was overwhelming and too much and...perfectly Hutchins.

Once the guys had settled in, and she'd gotten the explanation that Rafe had bribed the nurses on the floor with treats so they could all come in together, at least for a few minutes, the big conversation settled into smaller, side conversations, with Jer sitting at her side, stare locked onto hers.

He squeezed her hand. "You scared the shit out of me, Cor."

She squeezed back. "I'm the only girl. I've got to go big or go home."

"About the—" His eyes flicked down. "Are you okay?"

"Honestly? I didn't know I was...pregnant." She sighed. "But I'm sad anyway."

"Cor," he whispered. "I'm so sorry."

She forced a smile. "Me, too. But I'll be okay."

"You don't have to be tough, honey. We can talk about it, about what you're feeling," he said, glancing around the room. "We're all willing to discuss and—" He broke off, frowning.

"What?"

A shake of his head. "Nothing."

"*What,* Jer?"

"Rafe—"

Her gut clenched. "He's got nothing to do—"

A chime blasted through the speaker behind her head, the same slightly musical tone she'd heard several times over the past couple of days, announcing that someone should return a page or was needed in a patient room or at the nurse's station.

She winced, started to ignore it, and finish her thought.

But the voice came on.

And it was a voice she recognized.

"Attention. Attention, Hutchins clan."

"What th—" Jeremy's eyes went to the speaker in the wall.

She was already sitting up, and she twisted, which hurt less than she expected. Probably because the man was still talking and what he was saying had her even more on edge.

"That's—" She began loudly.

Jeremy leaned over, gently covered her mouth with his hand.

Normally that would have sent her straight over the edge...or at the very least, she would have licked his palm for the indignity of covering her mouth.

But Rafe was still talking.

And the room...the room fell silent.

"...Attention, Hutchins clan," he said again. "This is Rafe, your resident adopted son and annoying older brother, and the man just trying to be the best friend possible, and...I love Cora. I love your daughter, and your sister, and I need to make sure she knows that because she is the most important thing in my life."

Her pulse had sped up, thundering in her ears so loudly that she could barely hear all of what Rafe was saying.

"I made her think otherwise. I made *you* think otherwise, baby, and I was so scared of my feelings that I hurt you. But I love you, and I'm going to tell you that every day for the rest of your life, and I'm not going to waste another moment to show you that."

She wrenched her gaze away from the speaker, somehow knowing...

Knowing that he'd be in the doorway, that he'd be staring at her.

"But," she whispered, "my brothers—"

"Love you," Jeremy murmured, "and him."

Her eyes flicked to her brother's, saw that his eyes were warm, that he was smiling, not looking ready to murder the man she was in love with.

Gently, he pushed her cheek to the side, and she inhaled sharply.

Because Rafe was there.

His fingers came to her jaw, brushed lightly over the skin there. "I love you," he whispered.

"I—"

"And I love you enough, you *are* enough for me to make sure the entire world knows it." He leaned close, cupped her cheek. "Especially if that world includes your overprotective brothers."

She laughed. "But—"

"But nothing," he said. "I was a coward, like you said. I was too scared to see you, to see what we could be, and worse, I made you feel like shit because I made you feel like you weren't—"

"Enough."

His fingers flexed lightly. "Not enough. Not nearly enough.

This"—he snagged her hand, brought it to his chest, pressed it to the spot over his heart—"is yours. *This*"—he used his free hand, tapped his temple—"has finally got itself together, and so if you still want to give us a chance, still are willing to give *me* a chance, I—"

"Yes."

He blinked. "I didn't even finish the statement."

"Were you going to say I'd have your eternal servitude and I can always put my cold feet on yours and you'll always be the one to get out of bed to turn out the light when we forget? And—"

"Yes."

"Dude," Asher warned.

Her mom swatted him.

Hard.

"Ow," he muttered, rubbing his arm.

And Cora looked back at Rafe, saw his mouth had curved up. "Yes," he said again.

"You don't even know the rest of my list."

He leaned close, mouth brushing her ear as he spoke. "No," he murmured, "but I know *you*."

She shuddered, fingers threading into the hair at his nape, some part of her unlocking when he stayed close, when he nuzzled lightly at her throat, when his lips brushed hers.

"Get a room," she heard Asher mutter.

Then she heard him yelp and a laugh bubbled up in her throat.

"Unfortunately," she said, loud enough for their audience to hear, "I think my list also includes a half-dozen idiots who are related to me."

"Hey!" Rome declared.

"Trouble is," she declared, ignoring him, "I love the big, protective lugs, and so I can't imagine my world without them."

"The thing is," Rafe said, "I love the big, protective lugs, too. They may be annoying—"

"Truly, that's uncalled for," Wyatt grumbled.

"But the funny thing is, I owe them my life," he said softly, and the room grew quiet, the muttering silenced, the air going just the slightest bit tense, "because they taught me how to accept love, and then they taught me that the biggest, most powerful gift of all is to be able to give that love to someone else."

Cora's eyes stung.

"So know that I love you, Cor. That I understand how precious of a gift it is." His lips brushed her forehead, one cheek, the other, her chin, the tip of her nose. "And know that I won't ever squander the gift of you again."

Now it was less stinging and more attempting to not sob like a baby.

"Rafe, I—" Her voice broke, and she found herself whispering. "What if my list is too long?"

"Never."

"But..."

"*Never.* Here's the thing. Someone really smart told me that as long as we love each other right that everything will be okay."

Her mom sniffed, and Cora glanced over, saw Rowan handing their mom a tissue before he glanced back at her, winked.

As she turned back, her gaze hit Jeremy's, and he grinned, mouthed, "I'm the someone really smart."

"And I know you love me right, too," Rafe said gently.

Her hand found his, squeezed tight. "Why?"

His smile hit her right in the solar plexus. "Minus the sappy stuff?"

"For this moment, minus the sappy stuff."

Gentle fingers intertwined with hers, warm, soft eyes

holding hers...and then filling with mischief. "Because you shared your Cheetos with me."

The laughter and joy that had been bubbling up inside her burst free.

And the best part?

No punches were thrown.

Because her brothers laughed, too.

Epilogue

Rafe

He walked up to the house, Cora's arm tucked through his.

She'd just been discharged that morning, and surprisingly, her brothers hadn't given him a hard time about being the one to take her home.

Surprisingly, they hadn't given him a hard time about *anything*.

Right, so maybe that wasn't surprising because it was the Hutchins way. Once you were in, you were in, and he'd been in nearly his whole life.

Still, he couldn't help but keep flinching every time one of them came close, half expecting a punch to be flying at his face for daring to touch Cora.

Which Wyatt, Jer, and company thought was hilarious.

Bastards.

But he *was* touching her, and he was doing it a lot because... he loved her, and he wanted to show that and—

They'd reached the front door.

Which opened before he could reach for it, swinging wide and revealing her friends.

"We've got the full Get Cora Healthy Kit, prepped and ready," Heidi declared.

"So long as it doesn't include stories of handcuffs," he muttered.

Cora snorted then winced and grabbed at her side. "Don't make me laugh."

"Don't bust out the handcuffs then."

She smiled up at him, and fuck if it wasn't like the sun hadn't just slid out from behind the clouds. Then she patted his hand where it was wrapped lightly around her waist. "I think you'll come to have a neutral to positive relationship with my handcuffs when all is said and done."

His cock twitched.

He told it to behave.

Then they were walking into the house, and he was starting to guide her to the stairs...but she was pulling away, turning toward the family room—

And he stopped dead.

"What is this?" he asked.

The room was filled...with his things. The collection of pictures he'd unpacked the other night and set on the mantel at his apartment, were hung on the wall. A blanket that Edy had bought him—blue and green plaid—was folded and laid over the back of Cora's couch. His TV had been swapped for Cora's and he knew that was the result of Rome and Rowan, who were standing in the corner, fiddling with cords, Cora's old—and much smaller—TV, sitting on the floor and propped against the wall.

His signed Gold hockey puck was perched on one of Cora's shelves, propped up by a set of thrillers he'd had signed by his favorite author.

He spun, saw his shoes lined up on the shoe rack, his jackets on the coat tree in the corner.

His coffee pot on the counter.

Keys on the little plate she kept on a table in her hall.

"What is this?" he asked again.

Cora was there when he turned back, smiling gently at him.

Then her hands were on his arms, his shoulders, his face. "This isn't an announcement over a hijacked call system"—she grinned, and he knew, *knew* the bribe donuts he'd given the nurses had really paid off, when she brushed her lips over his—"but I love you, and"—a sweep of her arm—"this is me showing it."

"By stealing your stuff," Asher said. "I don't know that—"

Wyatt socked him.

He shut up.

Cora ignored them all. Her eyes were on his. Her mouth turned up. "I stole your stuff, because your home is here, is with me, and my pain-in-the-ass brothers—"

"Hey!"

Laughter in her gaze. "My lovable and extremely sweet, but still giant pain-in-the-ass brothers, who aided and abetted me from my hospital bed—"

"And while we love you"—Jer called—"we don't want to live with you."

"Yeah, Cor," Wyatt added. "Watch out. He leaves his dirty socks on the floor."

He chuckled, shook his head.

Cora rolled her eyes.

"Just so you know, bro," Rome chimed in, "Cora's hair gets *everywhere*."

"Boys!" Edy snapped.

"And, if we're going for full-disclosure, if you're living here, you're going to have to deal with us over all the time," Heidi said.

"We're not over *all* the time—"

"She's lying," Kels stage-whispered.

Cora rubbed her forehead. "Why did I decide to do this in front of an audience?"

He grinned, wrapped his arms around her waist. "Because they're our family."

"Because we're awesome!" Heidi hollered.

"Children," Edy snapped.

Their audience quieted.

"For the record, I also leave my dishes in the sink without washing them for a ridiculously long time."

"For the record," he murmured, smoothing back her hair, "I already know that."

"And I don't promise to always share my Cheetos." A beat. "Especially if I'm on my period."

He grinned. "That's fine." His lips found her ear, pressed lightly. "I don't even really like Cheetos, anyway. But your croissants, those you'll have to always promise to share."

A sigh, her hands on his jaw, one drifting down to cross over his heart. "You drive a hard bargain."

"I'll do the dishes."

She grinned, leaned up on tiptoe, whispered. "Just saying, Rafe baby, I don't really care about the dishes."

He turned his head so that his lips met hers for a brief kiss. "And I don't really care about the croissants."

Laughter and love in her eyes before she kissed him.

Before she pulled back and said, "Are you ready for this?"

"Ready for what?"

"Ready for the rest of our lives." She grinned. "And that starts with..."

"Game night!" Asher said.

"Our families. Us," Cora corrected. "And copious amounts of competition."

He leaned close, rubbed his nose against hers. "And yelling

and sabotaging and cheating." A beat. A kiss to her jaw. "Oh, and maybe love, too." Another kiss to the tip of her nose. "Because in this family, they go hand in hand."

Cora released him, weaved their fingers together, and tugged him toward the dining room.

Where there was a stack of board games a foot tall.

Waiting for them.

Waiting for him.

Waiting...

No.

He was done waiting. He was ready to live.

Which was why he grabbed *Catan* from the middle of the stack and declared, "You're all going down."

Catcalls. Boos. Hisses and shit-talking.

And family.

Thank you for reading! I hope you loved Cora and Rafe as they navigated sharing Cheetos, that special hot cocoa, and all those over-protective brothers! The next book in the Billionaire's Club world is BAD REBOUND, book one in the Billionaire's Club: Bad Brothers series. Watch the first of the Hutchins brothers fall...and then enjoy the sparks when Teresa's heels stay firmly on the floor!

CLICK HERE TO READ BAD REBOUND>

And if you enjoyed BAD BEST FRIEND, you'll love the small town of Stoneybrooke, its swoony heroes, and the klutzy, lovable heroines who steal their hearts. The first book in the series, TRAIN WRECK, is free to download!

"I laughed out loud all the way through the book, except perhaps during the sexy scenes. I'm not telling you what I did during

those." —Amazon reviewer

The more she falls for Stefan, the more she risks her career... Don't miss the Gold Hockey series. It begins with the over 400 five-star-reviewed BLOCKED!

"Off-the-charts hot, smexy scenes with one of the best book boyfriends I have come across!" —Amazon reviewer

DOWNLOAD BLOCKED FOR FREE >

I so appreciate your help in spreading the word about my books, including sharing with friends! Please leave a review on your favorite book site!

You can also join my Facebook group, the Fabinators, for exclusive giveaways and sneak peeks of future books.

SIGN UP FOR ELISE FABER'S NEWSLETTER HERE: https://www.elisefaber.com/newsletter

Excerpt from Bad Rebound

JEREMY

"Fuck, yes, I win!"

God, she was frustrating.

Gorgeous.

But frustrating.

Teresa tossed her head back and laughed loud and deep, showing off the innate confidence she had. She was a woman who liked what she liked, who lived big and unafraid.

And she was fucking intense when it came to any form of competition.

Brutal.

As in, she took an opponent down with precise strategy and absolutely no sympathy.

Case in point...

His utter destruction at her hands in spoons.

"I'm out," he muttered, tossing his cards—and let it be noted, he couldn't toss his spoon on the table because he'd lost...again.

Teresa had showed up about the time the board games got really serious and had jumped right in, just like she always did.

In the three years she'd worked for Rafe, she'd become an honorary Hutchins.

At Sunday dinners.

At game nights.

At family events and holidays and birthdays and—

She was there.

Always.

And...she was hot and sexy and gorgeous, and he wanted her.

But she was seeing someone.

So, he stayed away, kept his distance, rolled his eyes when she crowed, snarked back when she led with sarcasm, huffed out laughter when she threatened him...and generally acted the part of the annoying older brother.

Inside?

Inside he'd cataloged enough fantasies to write a dozen romance novels.

"We can play something else," Kate offered.

He shook his head, smiled at Cora's friend. "My eyes need a break. I'm gonna grab a beer."

There were offers to join him, but he waved them off, and in the end, it was just him who went out onto Cora's back deck, plunking into one of the chairs and holding his bottle of beer by the neck and staring up at the sky.

He'd finished nearly all of it by the time the slider slid open.

Footsteps on the deck.

He glanced up, expecting to see his twin, but it wasn't Wyatt clomping out on the wooden slats. It was...Teresa.

She looked beautiful that night.

Jeans, sneakers, a simple T-shirt. Her hair pulled back into a ponytail. No makeup.

No pretense.

Just...Teresa.

And she was the most beautiful woman he'd ever seen.

But she didn't seem to see him sitting in the corner of the deck, and in fairness, he'd purposely taken the area that was mostly in shadows because he'd just needed some time alone.

In the Hutchins family, there wasn't much for alone time.

Normally, he would have said something to announce himself, would have made some snarky comment just to have her snapping back at him. In fact, he'd opened his mouth to do so, but before he could, he saw it.

It.

She wiped her eye.

Then the other.

And fuck...was she crying?

He hopped to his feet. "Teresa?"

She jumped, spinning toward him, and clamping a hand to her chest. "What the fuck, Jeremy?"

He was moving already, hauling ass toward her, fingers coming to her jaw, turning it toward the lights, and yeah, *there*. Her eyes were damp, tears glistening on the ends of her lashes. "What's the matter, T? Who hurt you? I'll—"

She huffed out a laugh, shook her head. "You can't help but be an older protective brother, can you?"

What he felt for Teresa was the furthest thing from brotherly as there was.

"This isn't about me, baby." He slid his hand to her nape, holding her in place. "This is about why you're crying."

"As I said, I have plenty of older brothers. I don't need you to join their ranks."

His fingers flexed. "What. Happened?"

A sigh. A roll of her eyes. "Seriously?"

He just held her stare.

She sighed again. "For fuck's sake. It's nothing, okay? Sam broke up with me. That's all. My ex-boyfriend is an asshole and—"

"Did he hurt you?"

Teresa glanced over his shoulder. "He dumped me," she muttered. "It's not like that feels good. Not that you'd know *that,* considering you're so fucking hot girls are throwing themselves at you."

"They don't throw—"

"That bartender in the restaurant?"

"It wasn't like that. She just wanted some advice on her—"

"I know you're not going to tell me she wanted advice on her golf game now, are you?"

"She just—"

"Needed help with her backswing?" Teresa tapped a finger to her lips, drawing his focus there. Fuck, but she had the most kissable mouth. "Or was it back *seat* that she called it?" A smirk. "Probably because she was desperate to get there with you—"

"T."

"And how about the waitress who slipped you her number, and the jogger who pretended to twist her ankle, and the—"

"*T.*"

"And—"

"Teresa."

She blinked, looked up at him. "What?"

"You ever wonder why I never took any of them up on their offer?"

"What?" she asked again, this time in a whisper.

"You," he said. "You're the reason I never accepted any of them."

"What?" Another whisper.

"I like you, Teresa. I like you a lot."

"I...but—"

"But you've been dating someone, and I don't—I'm not the kind of guy who—"

"Who what?"

"Who fucks around on someone else's woman."

She sucked in a breath, released it slowly. "But I'm no one else's woman."

"No."

Wide blue eyes on hers.

"You're mine."

Her lips parted.

And...he just had to taste her.

So...he did.

CLICK HERE TO READ BAD REBOUND>

Want a free bonus story? Hate missing Elise's new releases? Love contests, exclusive excerpts and giveaways?
Then signup for Elise's newsletter here!
https://www.elisefaber.com/newsletter

And join Elise's fan group, the Fabinators https://www.facebook.com/groups/fabinators for insider information, sneak peaks at new releases, and fun freebies! Hope to see you there!

Billionaire's Club

Bad Night Stand

Bad Breakup

Bad Husband

Bad Hookup

Bad Divorce

Bad Fiancé

Bad Boyfriend

Bad Blind Date

Bad Wedding

Bad Engagement

Bad Bridesmaid

Bad Swipe

Bad Girlfriend

Bad Best Friend

Bad Rebound

Also by Elise Faber

***Billionaire's Club* (all stand alone)**

Bad Night Stand

Bad Breakup

Bad Husband

Bad Hookup

Bad Divorce

Bad Fiancé

Bad Boyfriend

Bad Blind Date

Bad Wedding

Bad Engagement

Bad Bridesmaid

Bad Swipe

Bad Girlfriend

Bad Best Friend

Bad Rebound

Bad Billionaire's Quickies

***Gold Hockey* (all stand alone)**

Blocked

Backhand

Boarding

Benched

Breakaway

Breakout

Checked

Coasting

Centered

Charging

Caged

Crashed

A Gold Christmas

Cycled

Caught

Cap

Breakers Hockey (all stand alone)

Broken

Boldly

Breathless

Ballsy (April 26,2022)

Love, Action, Camera (all stand alone)

Dotted Line

Action Shot

Close-Up

End Scene

Meet Cute

***Love After Midnight* (all stand alone)**

Rum And Notes

Virgin Daiquiri

On The Rocks

Sex On The Seats

***Life Sucks Series* (all stand alone)**

Train Wreck

Hot Mess

Dumpster Fire

Clusterf*@k

FUBAR (March 29,2022)

***Roosevelt Ranch Series* (all stand alone, series complete)**

Disaster at Roosevelt Ranch

Heartbreak at Roosevelt Ranch

Collision at Roosevelt Ranch

Regret at Roosevelt Ranch

Desire at Roosevelt Ranch

***Phoenix Series* (read in order)**

Phoenix Rising

Dark Phoenix

Phoenix Freed

***Phoenix: LexTal Chronicles* (rereleasing soon, stand alone, Phoenix world)**

From Ashes

In Flames

To Smoke

KTS Series

Riding The Edge

Crossing The Line

Leveling The Field

Scorching The Earth

Cocky Heroes World

Tattooed Troublemaker

About the Author

USA Today bestselling author, Elise Faber, loves chocolate, Star Wars, Harry Potter, and hockey (the order depending on the day and how well her team -- the Sharks! -- are playing). She and her husband also play as much hockey as they can squeeze into their schedules, so much so that their typical date night is spent on the ice. Elise changes her hair color more often than some people change their socks, loves sparkly things, and is the mom to two exuberant boys. She lives in Northern California. Connect with her in her Facebook group, the Fabinators or find more information about her books at www.elisefaber.com.

facebook.com/elisefaberauthor
amazon.com/author/elisefaber
bookbub.com/profile/elise-faber
instagram.com/elisefaber
goodreads.com/elisefaber
pinterest.com/elisefaberwrite

www.ingramcontent.com/pod-product-compliance
Lightning Source LLC
LaVergne TN
LVHW091133080826
845145LV00008B/2139

* 9 7 8 1 6 3 7 4 9 0 4 2 6 *